I0617783

Anthem

ANTHEM OF SURVIVAL

THOM COLLINS

Anthem of Survival
ISBN # 978-1-78686-388-1
©Copyright Thom Collins 2018
Cover Art by Cherith Vaughan ©Copyright December 2018
Interior text design by Claire Siemaszkiewicz
Pride Publishing

Published in 2018 by Pride Publishing, United Kingdom.

Pride Publishing is an imprint of Totally Entwined Group Limited.

ANTHEM OF SURVIVAL

Dedication

For my husband, Liam.

Prologue

It was the hottest ticket in town. *Lady Lynda*, the smash-hit musical at the London Palladium, starring Daniel Blake and Max LaFranchi. The critics dubbed them the Dream Team. Demand to see Daniel and Max in their limited twelve-week run had been phenomenal. The last chance to see the pair together in the show that had made headlines for the right — and the wrong — reasons. Tickets exchanged hands for hundreds, sometimes thousands of pounds more than their face value. *Lady Lynda* would go on without them, with a new cast of big names, but it wouldn't be the same. The Dream Team had captured the hearts of the capital.

The ticket frenzy for their final performance was like no other. The woman in the center of the stalls had paid almost two thousand pounds for her seat. It was worth it, she reasoned. Every penny. She had seen the show three times already, but she couldn't miss this. Not the last night.

The sense of expectation, of excitement was palpable as the auditorium filled around her. The audience was about to see a piece of history. No one had predicted the show would continue after its ill-fated run in Blackpool, when Daniel Blake had almost fallen victim to the murderer Sonny Rock. Sonny had killed twice already when he'd gained access to Daniel's hotel room, intending to kill again. But Daniel had survived and, against all expectations, announced his intention to play the role in London. He was a hero. Everyone wanted a piece of him. For twelve weeks and the price of a ticket, the public had their chance.

The woman in the stalls wanted more than a few hours of entertainment, or a firsthand glimpse of celebrity. Each time she saw the show, she took little notice of the story, the jokes or the catchy songs that had won the production a host of awards and five-star reviews. No. She fixed her attention on Daniel, nothing else. Watching, concentrating, planning. Totally focused.

She knew what she wanted to do. What she had to do.

The plan was already in place.

As the lights fell, and the audience went wild around her, she stayed still and quiet, watching the stage, waiting for him to enter. When he did, thirteen minutes into the first act, her hands, placed on her lap, tightened into fists. One glimpse of him was all it took to convince her.

The anger remained. Her hatred for him was still alive.

The pain she'd endured for so long had festered and hurt more than ever.

Daniel Blake did not deserve this applause. He had no right to the adulation.

Daniel Blake should be dead.
He soon would be.
She would make certain of that.

Chapter One

Daniel Blake, sitting on a shaded terrace in a pair of sun-bleached shorts, strummed a melody on his guitar. The afternoon sun blazed in a cloudless sky and, despite the protective canopy above him, the heat was intense. Beads of sweat ran down his neck, tracking over bronzed skin to the dark mass of chest hair. It glistened on his top lip as he gently chewed the bottom. With his eyes closed, he progressed through the strings. A moment later, he smiled, finally satisfied, and put down the guitar. He reached for the weathered notebook that had been his constant companion all summer and wrote in an eager, untidy hand.

Daniel had been working on the song for two days, both music and lyrics, and, at last, it was done. He had nothing left to add.

He lifted his gaze to the sky and inhaled full into his lungs. Across the terrace, the blue water of the Ionian Sea reflected the white light of the sun, its expanse an ever-changing collage of sapphire and diamond colors.

Down the coast, the outline of Corfu Island was a hazy mirage in the heat. This perfect view had been his for six amazing weeks. The idyll would soon be over, but not yet.

Daniel lay back on the lounger and lengthened his arms above his head, stretching the stiffness in his neck. He'd been so absorbed in the song, ensuring every chord and every word were right, he'd ignored his own comfort and now his body ached. A few weeks earlier, he'd made the mistake of writing beside the pool, in the direct glare of the sun, and paid the price. Two painful days in bed with sunburn. Since then, he'd stuck to the shade while working on his music. He lost himself so much in the process it was easy to burn.

Daniel studied his body as he lay there. He'd never looked so good or been this tan before. There'd been no time to sunbathe in the past, he'd always thought it a waste of time. He had had too much to do, too much to achieve, to spend his days lying around a pool. But he'd realized this summer that a tan didn't just suit him, it helped him feel better.

It wasn't just the sun. Daily sessions in the pool and long walks on the beach kept him in shape. Coming off *Lady Lynda*, he'd had every intention of letting his fitness routine go a little, if only for the summer, but it hadn't worked out that way. He was in better condition now than when he arrived, in mind as well as body.

His legs were strong, muscular and tan. He hardly recognized his own body. He inched down the top of his shorts to admire the contrast in color between the creamy skin below his waist and the coppery tones above. The villa was private and he could have bathed naked if he'd wanted to, except he wasn't that kind of guy. Besides, tan lines were sexy. He'd always thought so. Who needed to risk a burnt butt and balls?

The one thing that marred the bronze color of his torso was the scars between his hip bones and ribcage, sustained the night Oliver Gill had stabbed him, and from the lifesaving surgery he'd gone through afterward. Before coming to Corfu, the pale scars had been almost unnoticeable on his white skin. His dark body hair just about concealed them. But as his tan deepened, the scars stayed white, becoming more pronounced, forcing him to look at them, to acknowledge them.

Daniel traced his fingers along the lines and indentations. Had he made peace with the disfigurement? No. But as the summer came to an end, he'd learned to accept them.

Daniel sighed and basked in the heat. Life was not so bad, considering what the last two years had thrown at him. Better than that, things were good. Not perfect, too many questions remained unanswered for that, but his optimism grew every day.

The glass doors of the terrace opened behind him and Elijah Mann stepped out, offering him a cold bottle of water.

"It's hotter than hell out here," Elijah remarked, shielding his eyes against the sun to gaze across the sea.

Daniel swung his legs over the side of the sunbed and sat up. He drank the chilled, sparkling water and looked with admiration at Elijah's chunky thighs. While the sun had turned Daniel's white-boy skin an appealing shade of bronze, Elijah, with his Greek heritage, had gone nut-brown. The beige shorts and blue open-neck shirt he wore today complemented his tan. *God, he's gorgeous.* Daniel never had to remind himself what a lucky guy he was.

Elijah dropped onto the other sunbed, knees spread wide, and looked straight at him with soulful brown eyes. His thick blue-black hair fell in an untidy wave across his brow and a three-day beard darkened his jaw. With his natural Greek coloring, Daniel wondered if Elijah had ever looked more handsome. Even more important, he looked happier and healthier than he had in a long time. Less than a year ago he'd been in hospital, fighting for his life. Daniel wouldn't ever forget how close he'd come to losing him. Those long, terrible hours beside his bed, praying he would recover. Hoping for the best, afraid of the worst.

"How's it going?" Elijah asked, nodding at his guitar.

"I'm finished," he answered, smiling.

Elijah's eyebrows raised. "Really?"

"Absolutely."

"Don't keep me in suspense. Let me hear it."

"What's for lunch?" Daniel asked, feigning indifference.

Elijah leapt forward, grabbing Daniel's bare waist, tickling the sensitive flesh around his middle. Daniel yelped and fell backward, giggling. Elijah followed through, lying on top of him, fingers still working his waist. Daniel laughed, squirming against his hard body.

"No lunch today," Elijah said, his face on top of Daniel's. "Not until you play me your song."

"All right, all right." Daniel laughed, struggling beneath the weight of him. "I give in. You can hear it."

"As you surrender so easily, let me have a kiss too."

Elijah pressed his advantage, moving his lips on top of Daniel's, taking him in a deep, open-mouthed kiss.

Daniel gave in, thrusting his fingers into Elijah's dark, lustrous hair and drawing him in further.

He never wanted it to end. The kiss, the embrace, their time together. Alone in Corfu. No pressure, no commitments, no worries. They were safe here. Happy.

"Come on," Elijah said, drawing back at last. "Play me your song."

Daniel picked up his guitar and notebook and arranged himself on the sunbed opposite. He played and sang with no sense of embarrassment. Song writing was a new experience for him. He'd spent the best part of his career interpreting the words and music of other writers. Great writers and great songs, but after all he'd been through on *The Atlantic Anthem*, and last year in Blackpool, he'd struggled to find songs that expressed what he felt. He found it hard to connect with other people's stories and experiences. His emotions — his fears, hopes and anxieties — were unique to him. No one else could tell them.

Elijah had become the sounding board for his writing. The only person who knew what he'd been through. Who understood the confusion, panic and anger their ordeal had created. Daniel didn't know if he could share these songs with the world, if he even wanted to, but he could sing them to Elijah, as a catharsis for them both.

The song he'd just written was called *Watch Out For Dangerous Men*. The music and the melody were beautiful, at odds with the lyrics, which were full of antagonism and outrage. There was a 1970s pop vibe to the song, influenced by Bowie, 10cc and Billy Joel, his favorites from a time when music and melody had most meaning. It was rough, acoustic, he needed to work on the vocal phrasing and arrangements, but even now, singing it when it was still new, the song said everything he'd tried and failed to express on his own.

Elijah listened and Daniel noticed a slight furrowing of his brow at a couple of the lyrics, but otherwise he gave away nothing. Finished, Daniel put down the guitar and closed the cover on his battered notebook. Elijah looked at him with dark, glistening eyes.

"That's...incredible," he said at last. He swallowed. "You've been bottling all of that inside you?"

Daniel shook his head. "Not bottling it, no. Just looking for a way to express it. I didn't know how to say those things before. For the longest time, I didn't know what I wanted to say. It was caught, in here." He thumped his chest. "Something stuck, that I couldn't get out."

"Like an emotional hairball."

Daniel laughed. "Exactly like a hairball."

Elijah flipped sunbeds, sitting right beside him. He put an arm around Daniel's shoulder, pulling him close, until their heads touched. Daniel loved this, the closeness between them. He needed music to let the world know how he felt, he couldn't express it any other way, but with Elijah, he didn't have to speak, didn't need words. They understood each other completely.

"What's your intention for these songs?" Elijah asked. "They're too good to keep hidden. All that emotional rawness has to be shared."

"I don't know whether anyone wants to hear it. I've always been a covers artist. Singing good old favorites. Show tunes and classics. That's what people expect of me."

Elijah squeezed him. "You *were* a covers artist. Not anymore. You've got your own material now. Brilliant material. You should sing it. Share it."

"Maybe," he said. "We'll see. When we get back home, I'll record a few demos, see how it goes from there."

Elijah picked up his notebook and browsed through pages filled with Daniel's untidy scrawl. Ideas, crossings out, reworkings, fragments—his heart poured out between the lines. "How many songs have you written?"

"Probably around sixteen complete. And another seven or eight at various stages. Some of them may lead nowhere, but I think there are three potentially good ones among the unfinished stuff. Enough for me to work on."

"You've got enough here for an album," Elijah said. "Easily. A strong one at that. Why don't you play these to Ben? It's his field after all. Take his advice. Maybe he can help you to demo them."

"We'll see." Daniel took the book back from Elijah and closed it. "C'mon. I've done my part, sang for my lunch. What are we having?"

It was too hot to eat alfresco, even in the shade. Elijah set the table in the air-conditioned dining room, just inside the terrace where they could still enjoy the views, the sea on one side and the lush garden on the other, filled with indigenous plants and flowers. The villa combined traditional and modern architecture, casually elegant and spacious, with full floor-to-ceiling windows that flooded the chic interior with light. Daniel fell in love with the place the moment they arrived.

While Elijah sorted lunch, Daniel went to the ground-floor bathroom. He washed his hands and face and ran damp fingers through his hair. Even that had caught the sun during his time in Greece – its dark color was streaked with gold. With his light hair, sun tan, stubble and cleft chin, he looked more like a 1960s movie cowboy than ever.

He pulled on a lightweight shirt and returned to the dining room. The bracing air con was a blessed relief after the fierce heat of the terrace. They were deep into September and the strength of the sun showed no sign of abating. Elijah had set place mats, cutlery and wine.

"Need any help?" Daniel called into the kitchen.

"All sorted," Elijah answered. "Sit. Pour the drinks. I'll be right there."

Daniel reached for the wine, a traditional Raditius rosé, and poured two glasses. They must have drunk gallons of the stuff across the summer.

Elijah returned with a huge platter of food. There were skewers of breaded king prawns and a bowl of Greek salad made with green peppers, cucumber, olives, fresh mint and dill, with generous chunks of feta cheese. He'd already prepared a simple dressing of olive oil, lemon juice and black pepper. They could eat all of these things when they got home but it wouldn't be the same. The ingredients had come from a local market that morning. Part of Elijah's holiday routine was to get up early and shop for the best ingredients each day.

"This looks great," Daniel said, drizzling the dressing over the salad. "And it smells even better."

Elijah picked up two large wedges of lemon and squeezed them across the platter of prawns.

Daniel grabbed a skewer and attacked it with gusto. Juicy and succulent with a crispy coating, the prawns were delicious.

Since winning the TV show *Celebrity Top Cook,* Elijah's passion for food had flourished, offering an outlet for his energies in the aftermath of the assault he had suffered. Through the long days of his recovery, he'd lost himself in cookbooks, reading everything he could get his hand on, hungry to learn and expand his knowledge. Daniel encouraged him, buying him books and going out of his way to get fresh ingredients.

When the time had come to take a holiday together, Elijah had suggested Corfu. "My mother was born there, and we used to go back for family holidays throughout my childhood," he'd explained. "I've been reading a lot about the food of Greece and I want to experience it firsthand. To learn at source. You want to relax, I want a working holiday, this place has what we're both looking for."

The *Celebrity Top Cook* team had put him in contact with Kostas Paragios, a renowned Greek chef with an award-winning restaurant in Corfu Town. Kostas agreed to mentor him during his time on the island, allowing him to work in the kitchen four days a week. Daniel was unsure of the idea at first. He'd thought Elijah should take things easy. The stresses of a professional kitchen were far from relaxing.

"It's what I want," Elijah had assured him. "I promise I'll quit if it gets too much, but I have to do this."

Reluctantly Daniel had agreed, but had soon realized that his fears were unfounded. Elijah thrived under Kostas' tutorage. "The attack forced me to evaluate my life," he had admitted to Daniel one night. "Lying in bed gave me a lot of time to think. About where I'm going and what I want to do. Hell, in five years from now I'll be forty. If I'm going to make changes, there can be no better time than now, right? I don't want to be a comedian all my life. I've gone as far as I can in that direction. The competition awakened a passion for food I didn't know I had. I'm good at it and I love it. This is an opportunity I can't let go."

Looking at him now, and the food on the table, Daniel was proud of him. Elijah had proved himself. He'd seized his dream and made it his own. It was a triumph against Sonny Rock and whoever was behind him, pulling the strings. They'd tried to destroy their lives but had only made them better.

"Will you be sad to go home?" Daniel asked as he emptied his plate.

Elijah took a sip of wine and paused before answering. "No. It's been the best few weeks of my life, but holidays have to end sometime."

"It doesn't have to. We could stay. Buy a place of our own."

"No." Elijah's voice was soft.

"Why not? You said you love it here."

"I do. But it's not who we are. We have to go back. Work is there. Our families are there. Our home."

Daniel sighed. "Home. It doesn't feel like that anymore."

"You mean the house?"

He nodded. In the aftermath of the attack, the house they shared in Leeds had come under siege from reporters and photographers. He couldn't take out the bin without being photographed or having someone go through the contents of their trash. The attention was never-ending and relentless. During the London run of

Lady Lynda, the paparazzi outnumbered the fans at the stage door each night.

"I'm not looking forward to going back," Daniel admitted. "It's not the same."

"We can move if you want to," Elijah said. "It's only a house. We could sell it, or rent it out. Find somewhere else to live."

Elijah had a way of saying exactly the right thing. Selling the house would be a huge upheaval, but Daniel was already entertaining the idea. It might be the only way to get the fresh start they needed.

"Let's see how it goes," Daniel said. "Maybe I'll change my mind when we get back." Doubtful, but he would give it time.

* * * *

After lunch, they lay by the pool. The late afternoon sun had lost some of its intensity, but the temperature remained in the mid-eighties. They stripped to their shorts and relaxed in the heat. In a few days from now they would be back in England — back to the damp and the cold — they had to make the most of this Greek weather.

Daniel had settled into a comfortable routine during their time in Corfu. A lie-in each morning followed by twenty lengths of the swimming pool before breakfast. He'd spend most mornings working on his music before lunch. On the days Elijah worked at the restaurant, he'd spend his afternoons by the pool, writing or reading. He'd gotten through a long list of novels he'd never had time to read before. Some nights he had gone into town to meet Elijah from work and have a late snack. Others he had been happy to stay at the villa on his own, or walk to a nearby village to listen to live music in the bars.

He didn't go out as much as he wanted to. The paparazzi had finally caught up with him. A couple of times he had been on his own and the pictures had appeared in the press a few days later with stories about 'Sad Daniel' the 'Lonely pop-star haunted by tragedy.' Some nights it was easier to stay home than face the cameras and the stories that would be made up about him.

Elijah had worked his last shift in the restaurant. They had three more nights together before facing the reality of their journey home.

"What do you want to do this evening?" Elijah asked.

"Not a lot," Daniel said, turning his head to look at him. "I'm in quite a lazy mood."

"Suits me," Elijah drawled. "Let's get wasted."

Daniel laughed. "I like your thinking."

He went back into the house, returning with two cold beers. Elijah arranged his bed into a sitting position and took the bottle. It struck Daniel how thoroughly at home Elijah looked in the garden, in the realm of colors and scents and fresh sea air. With his dark skin and black hair, he suited the environment here much more than England.

The scars on Elijah's abdomen were a brutal reminder of reality. Like Daniel, his lower torso was marred by pale pink lines, crisscrossing his dark skin. Elijah's scars were far worse than his own. Sonny had stabbed him with greater ferocity than Oliver Gill's attack on Daniel. The surgery required to save Elijah's life had left him with a jagged line right across his belly. Daniel knew he was self-conscious about it and would only sunbathe without his shirt in the privacy of these grounds.

The paparazzi had yet to snap a picture of their matching scars, but Daniel knew from Keeley Rank there was a high price on such a photo. A handsome incentive for any photographer to keep up the pursuit of them.

The afternoon drew on. They drank a couple more beers, Daniel played another of his songs and they talked about their plans for going home as the sun dropped toward the horizon. Looking up at the sky, Daniel saw the brilliant hues of violet, red and orange.

"Let's take a walk before it gets dark," he suggested, pointing at the sunset. "It would be a shame to miss all this."

"Okay."

"Give me a minute first."

Daniel hurried to the house and their bedroom on the first floor. He changed out of his swimwear and into a pair of knee-length cargo shorts with deep pockets. The pockets contained a small can of mace, a personal attack alarm and a Taser. He never left the grounds of the villa without them, and would use them without question.

He'd been caught out twice before.

Never again.

For the rest of his life he would always look over his shoulder.

Elijah had put his shirt back on when he'd returned to the pool and stood gazing at the sea with a calm expression on his face.

"I'll miss this view," he said.

Daniel took his hand. "We can come back next summer."

"We might be working."

"We'll make time for it. Otherwise what's the point? Life's too short. We know that better than most people. Seize the day."

"Seize the day," Elijah replied, squeezing his hand.

They set off across the terrace, through a gate at the end of the garden and down a steep path that led to a private beach. They were quiet as they walked, comfortable with each other's silences.

Daniel breathed in the balmy scents of the evening, the strong odor of flowers bordering the path, the saltiness of the sea, the appetizing smell of meat and fish cooking in nearby restaurants. The sky was a near-perfect shade of violet when they reached the beach, and the water was as still as a mirror beneath. The small pebbled cove was cut off from the surrounding coast by high jutting rocks. The only access was from the path they had just walked down or the sea itself.

All through the summer, Daniel hadn't seen it look as beautiful as it did tonight.

They left their shoes on the beach and walked to the water's edge. Gentle waves washed around their ankles. Holding hands, they followed the contour of the shore to the far outcrop. A couple of fishing boats and a luxury yacht, about a mile off, were making for the distant line of the harbor, while farther out an enormous cruise ship had already switched on its evening lights.

Daniel wondered, as he often did when he saw a ship, where in the world *The Atlantic Anthem* was tonight. He thought about their days on the vessel a lot, but his memories were fonder now. He saw it as the place he and Elijah had met rather than where Oliver Gill had tried to kill him.

At the end of the beach, they leaned against the rocks, side by side, looking outward. Daniel inhaled and something stirred inside his shorts. This place, the evening, the man right next to him, they all had an arousing effect.

"What are you thinking?" Elijah asked.

Daniel smiled, turning to stand in front of him, still ankle deep in water. "Do you really want to know?"

"It's why I asked." He grinned back.

He took Elijah's hand and placed it on his groin, letting him feel the stiffness of his dick. He twitched against Elijah's fingers. "I'm thinking time is running out if we're to make the most of this beach and fuck beneath this sky."

"Shame we didn't think of that before coming down here," Elijah said, brushing his lips against Daniel's.

"I thought of it all right." Daniel reached in his back pocket and produced a small sachet of lube. "I'm always prepared."

Elijah wrapped his arms around Daniel, drawing him close. He put his hands on Daniel's arse, pulling their hips together. Elijah's cock swelled rapidly and Daniel ground against it. He thrust his fingers into Elijah's hair and forced his mouth on top of his, going in with his tongue, wanting all of him. After two years together, their passion for each other was stronger than ever.

Daniel couldn't get enough of him. His heat, his taste, his smell. The virility of his body, his wide shoulders, tight waist, his meaty arse. The length, girth and flavor of his cock. Daniel wanted all of him — all the time. He slid a hand between their bodies, gripping the meaty shaft of Elijah's cock through his shorts. He squeezed, feeling it grow harder.

Elijah groaned into Daniel's mouth and put a hand on the plump curve of his arse, leading him out of the water, farther up the beach. At the foot of the cliff, they stopped. Elijah pressed Daniel against the rock face and unfastened his shorts. They fell straight to Daniel's ankles and he stepped out of them. He was naked underneath. Cool sea air caressed the bare skin of his balls and his upward thrusting cock. Elijah took his dick in a firm hand and squeezed, milking pre-cum from the tip.

The sun had fallen below the horizon and Elijah stood silhouetted against a deepening purple sky. Daniel turned around and leaned his upper body against the cliff, giving Elijah free access to his arse. Before Elijah's injuries, they'd always been a versatile couple, taking turns fucking each other. Since his operations, Elijah had found it too painful to be on the receiving end, so this was the way it had to be.

Daniel didn't mind. He'd give everything to Elijah.

Giving up his arse was a pleasure.

He heard a tear behind him as Elijah ripped into the sachet, followed by the slippery wet touch of his fingers pushing lube into his arse. Daniel widened his stance and tilted his hips. Elijah's wet thumb pushed into him, going very easy. There was no need. Daniel was more than ready.

"Do it now," he growled.

Elijah put a steadying hand on his hips and drove his cock between Daniel's buttocks, locating the opening and entering. Daniel sighed and closed his eyes, thinking of nothing but the fullness inside. Elijah held him and pushed his big cock deep. Daniel was in ecstasy as the head slid against his prostate. It was the most agonizing but exquisite friction.

Elijah gave him everything he needed, long and slow. He put his chin on Daniel's shoulder and their heads touched as they fucked. They were never closer than like this, two bodies connected. They knew each other's rhythms. Daniel was close to coming but held back, controlling it till Elijah was ready too. They came together, Elijah's arms around Daniel, locking their bodies tight, shuddering through the raw pleasure of orgasm.

The world came back into focus. The waves lapping at the pebbled shore, the crickets and birds twittering on the cliff above them. Elijah's breath, hot against Daniel's neck.

The moment was perfect and couldn't last. Daniel knew that. But his experiences had taught him to live in the present.

He held Elijah deep and savored every second, knowing how lucky they were.

Chapter Two

"Daniel, darling." Max LaFranchi's unmistakable voice carried clear across the marina as Daniel and Elijah climbed out of their taxi. Shielding his eyes from the glare of the sun, he scanned the vast array of motorboats and yachts that were berthed there.

"Over here," Max hollered.

On a distant mooring sat a massive super-yacht, all white sleek lines and modern design. On one of the upper decks, toward the stern, a tiny figure waved madly in their direction.

Daniel waved back.

"A modest little craft," Elijah said, nudging Daniel's elbow as they headed along the marina toward the boat.

"Makes the *Royal Yacht Britannia* look like a tub," Daniel replied.

Max waited at the gangway, a huge grin on her face. She wore a patterned shift dress with flat gold sandals and a matching headband, keeping her light, sun-kissed hair off her face. There were flashes of her trademark jewelry around her neck and wrists.

"You look incredible," Daniel said, gathering her in his arms and lifting her off her feet. It was true. Toned and gorgeous, he'd never seen her look so relaxed or youthful. At fifty-six, she could pass for forty with no effort. She hugged him back and kissed his cheek. Her perfume smelled sweet and expensive.

As Daniel put her down, she immediately turned her attention to Elijah, covering him with kisses.

"My God," she said. "You get more handsome every time I see you. How the hell do you do it?"

"We've got portraits in the attic," Elijah joked. "The same place you hide your picture."

She laughed. "No attic required. I've got a sexy new husband to keep me young. Regular sex is the best beauty treatment I know. I wish I discovered it years ago."

"Where is Mr. LaFranchi?" Daniel asked.

"In the shower. He slept in this morning."

"Worn him out already, have you?"

"He can't keep up with me, I guess," Max said theatrically. "Come aboard. I've been dying to catch up with you."

They followed her up the gangway at the stern of the boat where a waiter in a uniform of white shorts and shirt welcomed them on board with a silver tray of champagne. Daniel smiled, taking a glass.

"I know you've got a diva reputation to maintain," he said, "but this is over the top, even by your standards. It must have cost a fortune." He saw several other uniformed crew members, their shirts emblazoned with the name of the yacht, *The Crystal Sea*.

Max sipped her champagne. "You boys don't know your divas as well as you think. A real diva never pays for anything. If they did, we'd be staying somewhere far cheaper than this." She chuckled. "The boat belongs to an old friend, Roman Di Pritzi. Do you know him?"

"We wish we did," Elijah said, casting his eyes around the state-of-the-art vessel.

"Roman's a terrific guy. Generosity should be his middle name. And kindness. He loaned us the yacht for our honeymoon as a wedding gift. The boat, crew, all our food and drink. Everything. There's an executive chef, a barman, a valet, housekeeper. Can you believe it? For six whole weeks we've wanted for nothing."

"Roman sounds like the man to know," Daniel said, impressed.

"C'mon, let me show you around. You won't believe it."

Max led them through the air-conditioned interiors of the yacht. Through a stateroom and dining room, a cocktail bar with its own sun terrace, a shaded reading room, three guest bedrooms and a huge master suite. Several times during the tour, Daniel caught amusement in Elijah's eyes, a slight smile playing on his lips. The boat was perfectly suited to someone like Max, a glamorous star with an image to maintain, but they could never be at home here. Sure, a night or two would be amazing, to experience how the other half lived, but it could never be more than that. It was a fantasy lifestyle.

They found Max's new husband, Ben Delaney, waiting on one of the upper decks, where a table was set for lunch. His cream shorts and open-neck shirt displayed muscular brown limbs. Ben smiled as soon as he saw them, well-known dimples framing his wide mouth. He ran straight at them, throwing his arms around Daniel and Elijah and pulling them into a group hug. He smelled shower-fresh and soapy.

"So good to see you," he said, squeezing hard.

"Don't leave me out," Max said, wriggling her way into the embrace.

They held each other in silence for a long time. Four friends who'd experienced more in a year than most people did in a lifetime. There was no need for anyone to speak.

Max and Ben had been married in a private ceremony in Italy, right after the London run of *Lady Lynda*. The wedding had been for close family and friends only. Daniel and Elijah had attended before going on to their holiday in Corfu, while Max and Ben had spent the summer honeymooning on *The Crystal Sea*, exploring the Mediterranean — Italy, Greece, Spain and the South of France. Some people were concerned when they had announced their plan to marry — Max and Ben had known each other only ten months — but Daniel knew better than that. The circumstances under which they'd met, the crisis in Blackpool, had created the kind of bond most couples never experienced.

"Ben is my soulmate," Max had confided to him one evening after a show in London. Daniel believed her.

Ben looked just as good as Max after their extended honeymoon at sea. The billionaire lifestyle suited him. Relaxed and carefree, their happiness was contagious.

With the tour complete, Ben gave instruction to the captain of the vessel that they were ready to set sail. With replenished glasses, they stood on the top deck and admired the view as the great craft exited the marina. It was another cloudless Greek day, with temperatures that threatened to peak in the nineties, but once the yacht cleared the headland and they were at sea, a cool breeze kept them comfortable.

"I've asked the captain to take us on a leisurely cruise around the island," Ben told them. "Sound good?"

"Perfect," Daniel answered.

Ben and Elijah went for a walk around the deck while Daniel and Max settled themselves on a sofa in the stern. Daniel slipped off his deck shoes and relaxed, enjoying the sea breeze as it ruffled his hair.

"Married life seems to agree with you," he said.

Max turned her face to the wind and sighed. "More than I ever imagined. After my first marriage went bad, I swore never again. No more commitments. Who needed it? It turns out, I did. I just had to find the right man. Ben treats me better than anyone I've ever known, but that's not all. We can talk to each other. Know what I mean? Really talk. I've never done that with a man before. My ex would tell me what to do but we didn't ever have a conversation."

Daniel knew what she meant. Max had been lucky enough to find her soul mate, the other half of her, and so had he. Looking down the deck, he watched Elijah and Ben as they leaned on the railing, enjoying the coastline. They were lucky to be here. If Sonny had succeeded, they would all be dead. But no, they were survivors, all four of them, and if being on this yacht was a little excessive, didn't they deserve some happiness?

Seeming to read his mind, Max said, "How is Joe doing? Have you spoken to the little guy lately?"

Joe Elliott, Daniel's dresser in Blackpool, was their hero. If it hadn't been for Joe and his smart thinking, Elijah would be dead. Ben too. If he hadn't alerted Daniel to the situation in his hotel room, he would have walked unwittingly into Sonny's trap. And when Sonny had Daniel on the floor, his hands around his throat, it was Joe who had pulled the trigger that sent the son of a bitch straight to hell. Joe hadn't escaped unharmed. Sonny had broken the boy's jaw before his campaign of terror was through.

Like Elijah, and Daniel before him, Joe's physical injuries had healed, but the psychological damage remained. In the aftermath, the Crown Prosecution Service insisted on pressing charges over Sonny's death. There was no way they could pin a murder charge on the boy, but Joe pleaded guilty to manslaughter. Daniel ensured he got the best representation when the case came before a judge for sentencing. Sonny was a murdering piece of shit, responsible for two deaths that they knew of, probably more. Joe did the world a favor getting rid of him. The judge agreed and sentenced him to a three-year suspended sentence. He didn't spend a single night in jail.

"He sent me a text the other day," Daniel told Max.

"How is he?"

"Good, I think. Okay at least. It's hard to tell from the message. But he's coming to visit when we get home next week. I'll get a better handle on him them. It can't be easy. I just want him to pull through."

"He will."

"I wish I had your confidence. I saw him before we came away and he's a shadow of the boy we used to know. He's only twenty-one, but with the attitude of a sixty-year-old. All his enthusiasm and vitality has gone. It's like he's given up."

Max looked at him earnestly. "Depression has a black heart. You know that as well as I do. We've both been through it. The recovery can't be rushed. Is he getting treatment?"

He nodded. "The doctors diagnosed post-traumatic stress disorder."

"Sounds right enough. I'm sure he'll be fine. Twenty-one or otherwise, he's a tough young man. He blew the head off that fucking psycho. That takes balls of steel and one hell of a strong backbone. Joe will get over this. He's made of the right stuff."

"I know. I still worry about him, though."

"And I'm sure he knows it. Having people who care about you is important. I'll look him up when I get home too."

"You don't have to. He's coming to the gala at the end of the month."

"He is?" Max's face lit up. "Perfect. We should do something to show we care."

"I don't think so. He won't appreciate a fuss. He's not ready for that. Not yet."

Elijah had been approached by a victim support charity to speak at one of their fundraisers earlier in the year. He understood the importance of such support networks and jumped at the chance, but after attending several of their fund-raising events, he wanted to do more. Now he had arranged his own fund-raising gala on behalf of the organization. In a couple of weeks they were heading to a country hotel where Elijah planned to cater a black-tie dinner. Daniel and Max had agreed to provide entertainment, and tickets for the event were priced at five thousand pounds per table of ten. That it had sold out weeks ago suggested they could have charged a lot more.

Elijah and Ben came back along the deck.

"Lunch will be ready at one," Ben told them.

"Time for another," Max said, raising her empty glass.

To Daniel's amazement, the white-uniformed barman appeared with a fresh round of drinks. *Where did he come from?* He accepted the new glass with a bemused smile. It was delicious and cold.

"How are you enjoying the high-life at sea?" he asked Ben. "Being waited on hand and foot must be a new experience."

"I'm trying not to get used to it," he said. "It'll be quite a comedown to go home and fend for ourselves."

"Takeaway dinner and boxed wine," Elijah said.

Max rolled her eyes in mock horror. "Boxed wine has no place in my life."

"It's grounds for divorce," Daniel said.

"You'd better ask your yacht friend the going rate for a personal wine waiter," Elijah said, patting Ben on the back.

* * * *

They ate lunch on the terrace on Deck Three. Daniel counted at least four upper decks though there may have been more. The yacht was huge. He'd worked on a couple of old ships that hadn't been much bigger than this thing. That Ben and Max were the only passengers seemed ridiculous. But as they had sailed around the island, they'd passed other super-yachts, which dwarfed this one. *How do people get so rich?*

Lunch was a delight of great food, excellent wine and the best company. Max and Ben told them about their European honeymoon, and the fantastic things they'd seen. They sat close together, often holding hands on top of the table and finishing each other's sentences as if they'd been together for decades. Their twenty-two-year age difference was irrelevant. In heart and soul, they were identical.

As the plates were cleared and coffee served at the end of the meal, Daniel sat back in his chair, feeling pleasantly full and satiated. It had done him good to get out. He'd spent so much time at the villa these last few weeks, alone or with just Elijah for company, he'd been in danger of becoming a hermit. The trip today had been just what he needed.

"How are things going with you and the poisoned dwarf?" Max asked him when they were done.

She meant Keeley Rank. Daniel had spent a large part of the last year working with the journalist and crime writer on a book about his troubles. Researching the history of Sonny Rock and Oliver Gill, looking for a link between the two. Keeley had told him right up front that she was two-thirds bloodhound when it came to finding the truth in a story. As far as Sonny was concerned, that had been true. Keeley knew all there was to know about him. His employment history and arrest record, she'd tracked down old girlfriends, past acquaintances, former victims and cell mates from his time in prison. Her dossier on Sonny was enormous.

She had the answer to everything except the most crucial question. Who had hired him to kill Daniel?

"What has she found out about Oliver?" Ben asked.

"Little we didn't already know. He was adopted, but the press was onto that before Keeley. His adoptive mother died about a year and a half ago. He had a sister. The police have ruled her out as a suspect though Keeley hasn't. She's still digging into her."

"They were close," Ben said. "Oliver and his sister. Well, as close as he was to anyone. She used to drive him around a lot in the early days. He treated her like an unpaid slave, taking advantage and talking her down. I think I met her a couple of times, but she didn't seem to mind him bossing her around."

"Is she a full sister?" Max asked.

"No. Adopted," Daniel answered. "My gut feeling is that she has nothing to do with Sonny. She's had it rough since the news about Oliver came out. Broken windows, dog shit through the letter box, getting sworn at in the street. Keeley still suspects her, but my instinct tells me not."

"Go with Keeley," Max said. "I can't stand the bitch but she's thorough. Don't rule out the sister until Keeley stops digging."

Daniel nodded thoughtfully. "I don't intend to. She's the expert at this kind of thing. I don't know how she finds out half the things she does. It can't be legal, that's for sure."

Elijah reached over and put a hand on Daniel's shoulder. "As long as she's on our side, we don't have to worry."

"What about Oliver's birth family?" Max asked. "Did she find anything there?"

"Nothing," he said. "He was dumped on a doorstep when he was a few hours old. His real mother was never found. Never made contact later."

"It seems unlikely that a woman who abandoned him as a baby would hire a hitman to avenge him as an adult," Max said. "Not without coming forward before now. She ignores him for, what, thirty years then decides he's worth killing for?"

"There's no one else?" Ben asked. "No boyfriends? Girlfriends? Obsessed fans even?"

Daniel raised his hands and shrugged. "He was a loner. Neither Keeley nor the police have found anyone with a significant personal connection to him. His friends were all fair-weather types. He was into the party scene — casual sex and drugs. People seemed to know him for short periods and then moved on. There was no meaning or purpose to his life."

"Do not feel sorry for that piece of shit," Max said. "He was a killer. A murderer. And two more people died because of him. Three if you also count that loser Sonny. Save your sympathy for Anouska, Luke and Christian. They're the ones who deserve it."

* * * *

For a second consecutive evening, the sun set in glorious fashion over the Greek Isles. Daniel and Ben sat on the running board at the rear of the yacht, trailing their feet in the cool water. *The Crystal Sea* had anchored a mile off shore. From their position Daniel could see the pale outline of their clifftop villa.

"It's been good to see you, man," Ben said, gazing out to the horizon.

Daniel nodded. Since Blackpool, when Ben had come back into his life after years, they'd been in constant contact. The six weeks this summer were the longest they'd been apart in that time. They were friends now, best friends, in a way they'd never been when they'd been younger. Daniel used to get along with Ben in the Overload days, but it wasn't like this. Their ordeal in Blackpool had formed a bond between them that wouldn't be broken again.

"I want to ask a favor," Daniel said.

"Anything, bro. You know that."

"I've been working on some songs." Daniel told Ben about his writing efforts, how he'd poured his heart into the lyrics. "Elijah says they're good. They feel right to me when I sing them, but I'd like your opinion. You're the professional. I thought we could spend a few days going through them together when we get home. I want to know if I could make an album out of them."

"It'd be an honor. Though I doubt you need me. You're a singer. You know more about a great song than I do."

"I'd like you to produce too. If they're good enough to record, I want you to oversee it."

Ben smiled, looking at him sideways. "It's my lucky day."

"What?" Daniel asked.

"Max asked me the exact same thing. She wants to make an album too. That remix she put out from *Lady Lynda* was huge. She wants to do a new CD in that style. Dance-diva kind of stuff. All original tracks. She's asked me to help her find the right material. Maybe we could write something for her. Me and you. What do you say?"

A warm surge of emotion rose through Daniel's body. He appreciated, more than ever, how fortunate he was. To have friends like this and a man like Elijah. To be so loved.

They sat for a while longer, enjoying the evening, the gentle roll of the boat, the rhythmic slap of small waves against the hull. The peace.

"Doesn't it bother you?" Ben asked at last. "That we still don't know who ordered the hit on us."

"Yes," he said. "It does."

"And, like, why haven't they tried again? It's nearly a year later and there's been nothing. No threats. No warnings. The bastard can't have quit. They can't have given up on us."

"No," Daniel said quietly. "They're biding their time, that's all. We're not dealing with an idiot, or some impulsive hothead. This is someone very clever and very patient."

"Doesn't it drive you insane? Not knowing."

"I can't let it. When the endgame comes, I need to be ready. Just as calm and as cold as they are."

Ben looked at him. "Can you do that?"

"Absolutely," he answered. "There's only one way this can end — with one of us dead. Me or them."

"But we don't know who they are."

"We will. There'll be no hitmen this time. No hired gun. It's too personal now. They'll show themselves eventually. And when they do, I intend to be ready."

Chapter Three

After six weeks of working in the restaurant kitchen, it was a shock for Elijah to sit out front as a regular customer. As the staff hurried around the terrace, taking orders and bringing delicious-looking plates of food to the tables, he couldn't help feeling like a slacker. Part of him wanted to rush into the kitchen, grab an apron and pull his weight with the rest of the team. But he couldn't. Not tonight. He was a guest of the house. He had to accept their hospitality with the same grace with which it had been offered.

It was their final evening in Corfu. This time tomorrow, their perfect holiday would be over.

Elijah kept a firm hand on his emotions. He had to. He'd lose it too easily if he didn't. This town, this restaurant, had thrown him a lifeline just when he had needed it. They were an essential part of his recovery. For both his mental and physical health, working here had been the greatest therapy.

Daniel's songwriting had provided a crucial outlet for the negativity that threatened to envelope them in the aftermath of Blackpool. Daniel was angry. Elijah understood that. Anger was a quiet, insidious emotion that must be purged. In the very beginning, after the attack on the *Anthem* and Anouska's murder, Elijah had been angry too, but last year, when he came around in the hospital following extensive surgery on his abdomen, he no longer felt it. It was an unnecessary emotion. Gone. Banished. Without it, he was ready to move on, to embrace life again.

Daniel wasn't there yet. Elijah understood. He had more reasons than anyone to be enraged. He would get over it, with Elijah's help. He was already on the way. His songs, his willingness to share them and his enthusiasm to record an album proved he was looking forward. Daniel's reluctance to go home was clear, but Elijah knew with absolute certainty what they had to do. They'd built a protective cocoon around themselves this summer. It was time to step out of it.

They sat at a table in Kostas' restaurant, in one of the arched arcades of Spianada Square, drinking martinis as they watched people go past. It was another balmy evening and the bars and cafés of the square were packed with tourists. Peak season had ended. At the turn of October, the weather would worsen and tourist numbers would decrease.

Elijah was ready to go home. The last six weeks had been perfect, but it couldn't last. If they stayed, it wouldn't be the same. As much as he loved it here, and the personal connection he had with the island, they were tourists the same as the others. This wasn't their home. England was.

"You look a little sad," he said to Daniel.

Daniel stared across the square, at the families, the children, their smiles and happiness. He exhaled at length. "A little," he said. "But only because it's over."

"There are plenty of things to look forward to. There's the gala in a couple of weeks. And you've got a whole album of songs to record. You won't have time to miss this when we get home. You'll be way too busy."

"I know," he murmured.

Elijah looked at him closely and saw the tense furrows between his eyebrows. He knew Daniel well enough. This was more than end-of-holiday blues. He reached across the table and took Daniel's hand. "What else?"

For a moment Daniel said nothing, then turned his blue eyes away from the people in the square to look at him directly. "A bad feeling. I can't shake it."

Elijah moved his chair nearer. "About what?" he inquired, his voice soft.

"It's irrational, I know, but I can't help feeling that once we get back, it will start over again. They, whoever they are, are waiting to make their move. They've been waiting and planning, all this time, and now they're ready to strike. They'll get us at home."

Elijah squeezed his hand. "Remember what we said last time? When I came out of the hospital. That we wouldn't live in fear. That we had to get on with our lives. And we did. You went back to the show, and I began to study. We didn't let it stop us then and we won't now."

"But they're still out there."

"And we take precautions, don't we? We won't be an easy target this time." Daniel had told him about the illegal Taser he carried all the time, together with a can of mace. Elijah also knew there were five other Tasers hidden about their house. And Daniel kept a baseball bat under his side of the bed and another in a downstairs cupboard, and he had an eight-inch butcher's knife in his underwear drawer. They had a burglar alarm, a panic alarm and CCTV around the house. He couldn't imagine anywhere safer or better protected than their own home. It was locked up tighter than Fort Knox.

"I know. We've been victims before but never again. This time it's gonna be a fight. And the second the fuckers shows their hand, it'll be all-out war."

Elijah hated to hear him talk like this. About fighting and war. It wasn't in his nature. He'd always been a kind soul. The most gentle man Elijah had ever met. Circumstances had changed him. Made him harder and more defensive. Elijah had changed too. He acknowledged the fact. He used to be laid-back and carefree, a tomorrow-is-another-day kind of man. A brush with death had made him realize that the opposite was true. They had to grab each day and live it like the last.

"There'll be no fighting tonight," he said. "Come on, we've got to make the most of this."

He signaled the manager, Dimitra, that they were ready to eat. Dimitra, the wife of the chef and owner, Kostas Paragios, led them to a table in the air-conditioned interior. While he loved to watch the world go by in the square, he preferred to dine away from the crowd. Even here, in Corfu, they were both recognized often. Dimitra sat them inside one of the arched openings, where they could still look out, but were concealed from most of the passing crowd.

Dimitra made a fuss over them, bringing a bottle of white wine, together with olives and bread. She left them with the menus. "I'll be back soon for your order."

They both laughed. They knew the menu inside and out and had made their choice hours before coming. On their last night, they wanted nothing but their favorites.

"Surely, you'll be sad to leave this place," Daniel said, sipping the wine.

"Absolutely. I love it here. But it's ignited something in me too. It's inflamed my passion for food and cooking and I want to take that away with me. I've got no interest in comedy or going back to the stage. That's over. This is what I want to do. To learn and get better."

"What about opening a restaurant of your own?" Daniel asked. "There's a huge gap in the market for Greek food where we live. We've got a wealth of Italian, Indian, French and Chinese restaurants, but no one does anything authentically Greek. The late-night kebabs don't count."

Elijah laughed. "No, they definitely can't compete with Kostas. I do want a restaurant or maybe a café of my own, but that's for the future. I'd fall on my arse if I tried it right now. I don't know enough, about cooking or business. I need to train, to keep learning, become the best, before I even think about opening a place."

"You underestimate yourself." Daniel's blue eyes glittered in the candlelight. "Your food is restaurant quality already. People would totally pay for what you do."

Elijah chuckled, appreciating the encouragement. "That's just cooking for the two of us. Look around, this place sits a hundred and twenty when it's full. Even if I had a place half this size, that's a huge deal. I'm not ready for it."

"I think you're selling yourself short, but whatever you decide, I'm behind you. One hundred percent."

They ordered their favorite starters, sautéed chicken livers on garlic flatbread. The livers were cooked in garlic, brandy and butter. It wasn't the most sophisticated dish on Kostas' menu, but it was the most delicious. They devoured it with undisguised glee, mopping up the rich juices with bread.

"When you do get around to opening your restaurant, this should be a permanent feature on the menu," Daniel said as he cleared the plate.

They finished the white wine and asked for a bottle of red to accompany their main course. Daniel seemed happier as the staff cleared the plates from their starters. The mood of melancholy that had affected him earlier seemed to have gone, and he talked with some enthusiasm about going home, about catching up with his family, his mother, his sister, nephews and nieces.

Daniel was a home-loving boy. As much as he liked to explore the world, Elijah knew he couldn't stay away for long.

Their main courses arrived. They'd ordered the same. Kleftiko, a traditional dish of very slow roasted lamb and herbs, served with potatoes and carrots. Again, it wasn't the fanciest choice on the menu but Elijah knew the love and care that went into preparing it. The lamb would have been in the oven since early that morning and the taste would be sublime. Nowhere on the island did a better version of the Greek standard. The velvety red wine was a perfect accompaniment.

Over dinner, they reflected on how good the holiday had been for them. They were both in better headspaces than when they'd arrived. There were a few lingering anxieties. Elijah conceded they might never go away. They'd survived violent attempts on their lives, the consequences of which might stay with them forever, but they wouldn't be governed by it.

But one thing continued to bug him. A problem he hadn't been able to conquer.

Sex.

Sonny Rock's vicious assault had done serious damage to his intestines.

When Elijah was discharged from hospital, the doctors told him in very blunt language that sex was out of the question. "In time, you'll be able to make love to Daniel," the doctor advised, "but until your injuries are fully healed, under no circumstances are you to take a passive role in anal sex. No bottoming."

Elijah had laughed. He was in agony. The sutures were still in place at the time. Sex was the last thing he wanted to think about, let alone indulge in. "Don't worry, Doctor. That's not going to be a problem at all."

"You'll be surprised," the doctor told him, "how quickly sexual urges return. I've seen patients get themselves in all sorts of trouble trying to have sex before their bodies are ready."

"Trust me," Elijah assured him. "That's not going to happen with me."

Except the doctor was right. As Elijah spent time with Daniel, getting better, his desire came back stronger than ever. Once his stitches came out, Elijah found he could fuck Daniel without pain or difficulty. It was enough to begin with, secure in the fact that when at last he healed, they would return to a healthy and varied sex life.

Eleven months later, they were still waiting. His body was fine. Everything worked as it should do. The obstruction was all in his mind. A fear they could inadvertently cause some lasting damage. Daniel would never hurt him, he was always gentle, but Elijah hadn't been able to relax enough to go all the way.

He'd hoped these six weeks in the sun would remedy that but he was still waiting.

"It doesn't matter," Daniel said, reaching across the table to take his hand. "I must have told you that a million times. We still have great sex, don't we?"

"It matters to me," Elijah said in a hushed voice. "I want our sex life to be as full and varied as it was before. Otherwise, Sonny has won. It'll always be something he took from us."

"He took nothing," Daniel assured him. "I've still got you, that's all that matters. The other stuff will come back, eventually. Remember, it hasn't been that long."

"It feels like forever."

"Less than a year," Daniel assured him. "That's nothing. We've got the rest of our lives together. Fifty, sixty years, if we're lucky. When we're old men, you'll be so tired of me fucking you, you'll wish that I couldn't."

Elijah laughed out loud, but the emotion struck him in a deeper place. They'd never talked that far ahead. Daniel had meant it as a joke, to cheer him up, and it had, imagining them old, still horny and turned-on, wanting each other as much as ever. That's something no one would ever take from them.

"I like that."

"Good," Daniel said. "Stop stressing about the sex and it'll happen when it's ready. In the meantime, let me take care of you. Anything you want from me is all yours."

The look in his eyes as he spoke was so soft, so kind, so lovely, it caused tears to prickle Elijah's lids. He blinked them away.

At the end of the meal Kostas Paragios, owner and world-famous chef, joined them with his wife, Dimitra, for a glass of Greek brandy. Kostas was a stout and vigorous man, with silvery hair and a full beard. His skin was chestnut-brown and his dark eyes always seemed to have a friendly sparkle to them. However stressful it got in the kitchen, Elijah hadn't once heard Kostas lose his cool with a member of the team. No swearing, no temper. A lot of professional chefs could learn from his quiet, intelligent manner. It was an attitude Elijah was determined to carry on into his own career.

Kostas and Dimitra had welcomed him like a member of their own family. Elijah would always be grateful for that.

* * * *

After dinner, they took an unhurried walk around the esplanade one last time. It had gone eleven but the bars and bistros were still packed. Couples and families sat on the terraces, drinking coffee and cocktails, and made the most of the laid-back glamor.

Elijah held Daniel's hand as they walked, unself-conscious and relaxed. They were no different from any other couple here. Just two lovers enjoying their last night on the island.

Except they were different. Few of these people would have had their lives threatened, not once, but twice.

Elijah had an uncomfortable feeling they were being followed. He didn't mention anything to Daniel. He'd been feeling it a lot lately. A sense of being watched. It was paranoia, nothing else. He tried to deal with it in his own quiet way. He'd sensed it almost every night when he left the restaurant and there was never anyone there.

No one followed him. No one stalked him. And yet, the feeling wouldn't go away.

"Let's stop for a minute," he said as they reached the citadel, breathing the night air and taking in the view. He looked around, vigilant, checking the people behind them. There were a dozen or so, taking the same route, all different ages, from kids to old folk. No one stood out. No one paying them any undue attention.

No one to worry about.

Would he even recognize the danger if it was there? In Blackpool, Sonny had sat right next to him in the theater bar, close enough to touch, to smell, and he hadn't had a clue. If someone was following them now, a professional tail, they wouldn't even know till he was upon them.

He swiped the idea away. It was the kind of paranoid thinking he warned Daniel against.

They had to get on with their lives. Without fear or obsession. Without looking over their shoulders the whole time.

"We should head back," Daniel said.

It was coming up to midnight. Their flight was in twelve hours.

Back at the villa, Elijah opened the doors onto the terrace. "Let's have a nightcap before we turn in."

"I'll get them," Daniel told him. "You go ahead, I'll follow you out."

Soft lights lit the garden and pool area. Beyond that, the sea was inky black, broken only by the twinkle of an occasional fishing boat or cruise ship far offshore. Elijah took a seat on the terrace and inhaled the fragrant night-time scents of the garden.

When Daniel joined him a few minutes later, he'd taken off his shirt. His toned, honeyed torso was a feast in the low light from the pool.

"You look like an Olympian," Elijah told him, accepting a glass of brandy. He gazed appreciatively at the hairy expanse of his chest and the clean lines of his torso and hips.

"This time tomorrow, we'll be in temperatures a lot cooler than this," Daniel said. "Make the most of it while you can. Tonight, it's shirtless. Tomorrow, I may need a sweater." He sipped the brandy and his lips glistened.

Elijah stood up, faced him, and unbuttoned his own shirt, letting it fall to the floor. Sultry air caressed his skin. Daniel put a hand on the small of Elijah's back, pulling him close. Their hips and bellies touched. Elijah moved in for a kiss and tasted brandy. His pushed his tongue into Daniel's mouth, wanting more, going deeper. He moved a hand to Daniel's meaty arse, squeezed the flesh and drew their hips tighter together. Elijah's cock came up hard and ground against Daniel's erection.

Passion and lust consumed them. Elijah followed the firm line of Daniel's jaw with his lips, to his neck, his throat, kissing, licking, breathing him in. Blood rose in a wave through his body.

"I want you to have me," Elijah moaned, his mouth against Daniel's skin. "Here."

Daniel squeezed Elijah's backside. "Are you sure?"

"Certain." He sighed. "Do it now."

Daniel spun Elijah to face away from him and reached around to unfasten his trousers. Elijah's heart raced as Daniel yanked them down with his underpants in one firm action. As they fell around his ankles, he stepped out and kicked them away. Completely naked, his body belonged to Daniel.

Elijah shivered, breaking into gooseflesh as Daniel placed gentle hands on his bare waist and pressed his lips along the nape of his neck. He leaned on Daniel and pushed his buttocks against his pelvis. Though Daniel still wore his trousers, his bulging cock nestled in the crack of Elijah's arse. Daniel pulled him tighter, letting Elijah feel the full force of his arousal.

Then Daniel maneuvered him toward the sunbed. Realizing his intention, Elijah climbed onto it, face forward. He lowered his head and shoulders and raised his arse in the air, finally offering himself.

"That's a beautiful sight," Daniel murmured behind. "More beautiful than anything else on the island, because it's mine."

Elijah gasped aloud and shuddered as something wet dribbled into the warm cleft of his butt. As Daniel stuffed his face between his cheeks and slurped greedily, Elijah realized that he'd poured the glass of brandy over his arse. He growled with satisfaction as Daniel's eager tongue skittered up and down his crack, shivering with fresh pleasure as it grazed his hole.

"God," Elijah gasped. "This is the only way I want to drink brandy from now on."

"Good idea, huh?" Daniel's words were muffled by his butt cheeks.

"Ingenious," Elijah sighed, raising his arse higher, opening it further. "Keep going."

Whatever Daniel was doing back there was working. Elijah's body relaxed, and his hole eased in a way it hadn't since his operations. Maybe it was the liquor too, numbing the opening, but he was keener to be fucked than ever.

The hunger he had for Daniel was all-consuming. He wanted him now. "I'm ready," he said, wriggling his hips. "Let me have it."

"Then stay right as you are," Daniel told him.

He heard Daniel rise, and the soft rustle of his trousers falling. The smooth slip of his underpants coming off, then the tear of a lube sachet.

"Tell me to stop at any time," Daniel said.

Elijah nodded, ready. Daniel touched his butt hole with just the tip of his finger and ran cold lube around the rim. Elijah raised his hips, encouraging him. Daniel entered, taking his time, only a centimeter before pausing. Elijah breathed deeply, but his body tensed.

No. No, I want this. I need it.

"Keep going," he said through gritted teeth.

Daniel pushed a little deeper. One inch, two inches.

Elijah's sphincter snapped tight around Daniel's finger, locking it in a vise-like grip. He cursed. There was no pain, so why should his body betray him like this? No way Daniel could progress further.

"Dammit. I'm sorry," Elijah said as Daniel withdrew from him. "I don't know what's wrong with me. I want you so much."

"There's nothing wrong. You're not ready, that's all."

"But I am ready," he said, rolling onto his back. "I want you to fuck me."

Daniel stroked his thigh. "Listen to your body. It'll know when you're ready, and when it is, everything will be fine."

Daniel moved his hand to Elijah's groin. He cupped his balls and squeezed until his softening penis hardened again.

"I want to make you come," Elijah said, rising to a sitting position on the end of the sunbed. He pressed his face against Daniel's balls, nuzzling them and feeling the weight and heat of his shaft across his nose and brow.

"You make me come all the time," Daniel told him, pushing fingers through Elijah's hair, guiding his mouth toward his dick.

Elijah tongued the thick root. "Come hard for me. I want to taste it." He reached for his own untouched brandy glass and passed it to Daniel. Then he gripped the base of Daniel's shaft, raising the head. Daniel held the brandy above, teasing, tipping slowly, until a few drops of amber liquor splashed upon the tip. Elijah dived for it, taking Daniel's cock in his mouth, tasting skin and brandy, a potent combination.

He backed off, his mouth open, Daniel's cock on the tip of his tongue. His anxiety of moments earlier forgotten. This was a different trip. Daniel poured a more generous slug the second time. Elijah took it gratefully, sucking it off his cock. Soon there was a new flavor in his mouth — brandy and pre-cum. He sucked harder, drawing more of Daniel's natural juices to the tip. The strengthening taste caused him to renew his effort.

Daniel moaned. He was helpless. Taking Elijah's head in both hands, he thrusted into his mouth. Elijah relaxed, allowing Daniel to guide him, to control the stroke. Daniel's legs trembled, each lunge becoming more erratic, until Elijah was rewarded with a hot flood of salty fluid, filling his mouth, obliterating the lingering taste of brandy.

He swallowed happily. Daniel's orgasm had brought the evening, and the summer, to a perfect end.

Chapter Four

They touched down in Leeds in the late afternoon. To Daniel's surprise the sun was shining as they exited the plane, though the temperature was several degrees lower than it had been in Corfu. He pulled up the zipper of his light navy jacket and they were waved through customs as priority passengers. An airport steward ushered them through to a waiting room as the luggage was brought from the hold.

"That's it then," Daniel said, "back on home soil. It's definitely over."

Elijah gave his butt a playful pat. "Only the holiday. There are plenty of new things about to begin."

He nodded, knowing Elijah was right. He used to love coming home after time away and would often spend the last few days of vacation looking forward to the familiar comforts of his own place. It was different now. Though he missed his family and couldn't wait to catch up with them, the prospect of going back to the house had no appeal. Not this time.

His anxieties were confirmed as their taxi turned onto their road and he saw eight photographers and a small group of fans waiting outside the gates.

"Shit," Daniel said, as he eyeballed the crowd. "The word must be out that we're back."

Elijah patted his knee. "At least they left us in peace for the summer. Mostly."

"Yep. But here they are, right on our doorstep."

Elijah used a fob on his keyring to open the electric gates. Daniel stayed stony-faced as they drove through and cameras flashed at every window of the car. They continued to click as Daniel and Elijah lifted their cases from the boot to the front door.

"Seriously," Daniel whispered. "Can these pictures be worth their bloody time? Two men taking luggage out of a car. Who wants a photo of that? It's hardly an editor's dream."

He knew the answer to his own questions. There were dozens of cheap magazines cluttering up the shelves of newsagents and supermarkets, all with pages to fill, week after week. Anyone with the most minor of public images was good for a feature or two. Anything to fill the gaps between the ads.

"C'mon." Elijah took his hand. "If we give them what they want, they'll probably go away."

"Until tomorrow," Daniel grumbled. He hated the pissy sound of his own voice and followed Elijah to the open gates where they waved at the press and the fans with their cameras.

In the past, he'd always made time for his fans. The people who bought his albums and came to the shows were the ones who made him. He would always meet them at stage doors and sign anything they requested. But since the *Anthem*, even more so since Blackpool, he'd noticed how he attracted a different kind of fan. Like this lot here today. The people who followed him around. Who turned up at the house. Who knew every detail of his schedule. They weren't fans.

Like Lauren Warwick, who stood across the road right now, filming every second of this on her phone. Lauren had been following him for about eight months. She seemed harmless enough at first, a big moon-faced girl, always smiling and pleasant. It didn't take long for him to realize how unhealthy her infatuation with him was. Together with another girl, she used to run a fan page and Facebook group, calling themselves Blake's Bitches, until he asked them to stop.

"That's an awful way to refer to yourself," he'd told them when Lauren and a gang of her friends came to watch *Lady Lynda*, wearing T-shirts emblazoned with the name.

"But we are your bitches." The group giggled.

This new level of inappropriate attention made him deeply uncomfortable.

There were several familiar faces hanging with Lauren today. The Blake's Bitches posse. He wished they'd find something more productive to do with their lives.

Despite Elijah's arm around him, Daniel felt vulnerable and exposed as they stood in front of the paparazzi and fans. It was wrong. They shouldn't have to make a spectacle of themselves outside their own home. He hated the fact they were defenseless too. He couldn't have risked bringing the Tasers or mace through airport security, so they were all hidden in his suitcase, out of reach. It was unlikely anything would happen with all these people around, but not impossible. Who knew if these photographers were all genuine? Any one of them could have a knife or, worse, a gun.

"Good few weeks away, boys?" asked one man without looking up from his camera.

"Perfect," Elijah answered, "but it's been a tiring trip home. We just want to settle back in and catch an early night. Don't waste your time hanging around, we won't be going out again today."

They stepped back and Elijah closed the gates. The paps seemed to take him at his word and packed up their stuff. The fans across the road were more reluctant to get moving. Lauren, with a huge pack on her shoulders, looked as if she had settled for the evening.

"I wish those kids would go," he said to Elijah as they headed for the front door. "I can't believe they get anything out of it, hanging around and watching a house."

Elijah unlocked the door and glanced back toward the street. "If they're still there in an hour, I'll have a word. Move them on."

"No," he said. "Lauren wants the attention, it'll only encourage her further. If she wants to waste an evening on the street, that's her problem."

They stepped inside and Daniel shut and locked the door, grateful to be home. Elijah turned off the alarm. "All good," he said, consulting the security panel. "No alerts."

Daniel was happier now they were inside, where all his security devices were in easy reach, but as he looked along the empty hall, his spirit sank. It was not good to be back.

Their housekeeper, Verona, had been through that morning. She'd put fresh flowers in a vase on the hall table, and the house smelled of vanilla air freshener.

She'd been coming in twice a week while they'd been away, so the house hadn't developed that cold, neglected feeling he hated so much.

He sighed, hoping he would settle in soon enough. They were home now. He had to get on with it.

"Why don't you make a pot of tea," Elijah said. "I'll take the cases up."

In the kitchen, there were more flowers. He'd arranged a grocery delivery for that morning too, so the cupboards and the fridge were full. He filled the kettle. As he waited for it to boil, his phone rang. It was Keeley Rank.

"Welcome back," the journalist said when he answered.

"How did you know we were home?"

"Your bitches of course. It's all over social media. Nice luggage by the way. Though you don't look exactly thrilled to be back."

Daniel groaned. Was nothing private anymore? It appeared not. "Keeley, we're barely through the door. The kettle hasn't even boiled yet. Whatever you want, can't it wait?"

"No. I need an answer from you now. Can you meet me in London the day after tomorrow?"

There was a note of urgency in her voice that he wasn't used to hearing. She was onto something. After all this time, had she at last made a breakthrough?

Daniel sat very still though something inside him tightened. "What is it?"

"Oliver's sister, Rachel," Keeley said. "She's agreed to meet us."

"What? I thought she wanted nothing to do with the book."

"That's what she's always maintained. She wouldn't talk about Oliver to anyone. Until now, it seems. She cracked this morning. I always knew I could break her. I don't want to give her time to change her mind, so I've fixed a meeting for Thursday. Can you make it? She wants you to be there."

"Of course." There was no way he'd miss this opportunity. Getting close to Rachel, Oliver's only known relative, had been at the top of their list all year. Rachel had refused every request for an interview so far. Daniel understood her reasons. Her world had been torn apart by her brother's actions. The press on Daniel's doorstep were small-time compared to the attention Rachel received. Every aspect of her life had been uncovered. Previous boyfriends, children, employment — nothing was off limits.

The police had found no link between her and Sonny Rock and eventually ruled her out of the investigation. Her hands were clean. And yet, she was the person who knew Oliver better than anyone. Maybe the only person who did know him.

It was essential that they talk to her.

"What brought about the change of heart?" he asked.

"No idea. I was as surprised as anyone to get a yes. I must have worn her down. I've been pestering her for an interview at least twice a week. I think she agreed just so I'd fuck off." She laughed throatily.

Keeley Rank had a thoroughly toxic reputation. From everything Daniel had seen of her, it was royally deserved. She was ruthless in her pursuit of a story — without empathy, pity or understanding — she would nail anyone for a juicy angle. The story was everything to Keeley. They were on the same side, so he had nothing to worry about for now, but she'd be an absolute bitch if working against him.

Keeley would never waste her time camping on a doorstep, like the journalists who followed him. She didn't wait for a story to come to her — she went out and grabbed it.

* * * *

Elijah was in the bedroom, sorting laundry into piles, when his mobile rang. He ignored it till the ringing stopped and continued what he was doing. Ten seconds later, the phone rang again.

Goddammit. Couldn't they have one night of peace before the calls began? He threw down a shirt and grabbed the phone, staring at the screen. It was April Evie, event organizer for Supporting Victims, the charity that would benefit from his upcoming gala night. Begrudgingly, he answered.

"April," he said. "I can't talk. We haven't been in the house five minutes yet."

"You've had a great holiday, I hope," she said, undeterred. She had a professional, cheerful-sounding voice, but despite every effort, she'd been unable to excise the last trace of her Liverpudlian accent. "I just want to give you an update on where we're at."

"The gala isn't until next week," he said. "This can wait till tomorrow at least."

"We're completely sold out," she went on, oblivious to his tone. This was not news. The tickets had all gone before he left for Corfu. "I've got people calling up, asking me to squeeze in more tables. I tell them we're already rammed to capacity and they offer triple and quadruple the asking price. This is such a hot event, people are ready to kill for a ticket." Then, realizing the tactlessness of what she'd said, she flustered. "I-I mean it's the social event of the year. The highlight of the charity calendar. Everyone's desperate to be part of it."

"It's great that Supporting Victims will make so much from this, but really, I don't need to know. I just want one quiet night at home with Daniel. That's all. I'll think about everything else tomorrow. Okay?"

Clearly it wasn't because she kept talking. "So, I need to get an order off to the printers soon and I'm calling to ask if you have the menu ready?"

"April," he said, losing patience. "Aren't you listening? I have literally just got home. I haven't finished emptying the suitcases."

"Oh." She sounded put out. "But I thought, well, you've had six weeks. Don't you know what you want to serve for this meal yet?"

"No. I've had six weeks of learning and relaxation. Thinking about food. I'll work on the menu over the next couple of days."

"But the printers—"

"Yes, yes, I know. The printers, the suppliers, the butchers, they all want to know. And they will. When I finish my holiday."

He hung up and turned the phone to silent. No more calls today. He was done until the morning. One more night with Daniel, that's what he needed, before the world intruded.

He found him in the conservatory. The French doors were open, and a fresh breeze blew in from the secluded garden. Daniel had put a pot of tea and cups on the table and a three-tier cake stand, loaded with scones, and pots of clotted cream and strawberry jam.

"What's all this?" Elijah asked, checking out the scones. They looked homemade, as did the gloriously colored jam.

"I found these in the kitchen. A welcome present from Verona. She must have baked them while she was here this morning."

"We don't pay her enough," Elijah said, cutting into a scone, which was filled with raisins and sultanas, before slathering it with jam and cream. *Delicious.* He adored the food of Greece and the Mediterranean, but there was nothing as comforting as an English cream tea.

"We'll have to hit the gym now we're back," Daniel said, pouring the Earl Grey. "I'll miss having a pool to swim in. I can't eat like this every day, not if I'm going to fit in my stage suits."

"We'll worry about that tomorrow. For now, let's just relax and enjoy."

Daniel's mood mellowed as they drank another cup of tea. Elijah had seen how edgy he'd become since getting back. The tension in the car from the airport had been palpable. And when they spoke to the photographers, Daniel had been like a tightly wound band, ready to snap. The benefits of their time away would be undone if he didn't calm down.

Maybe it was this environment after all, and coming home hadn't been such a good idea. Daniel had been saying for a while how he didn't feel safe here. Elijah thought they'd overcome those anxieties. Nothing bad had ever happened in this house. It was secure. Their own fortress.

They'd always been happy here.

He hoped they could be again.

* * * *

They spent a quiet evening together, ignoring the phone when it rang. They stayed in the conservatory most of the time, away from any prying eyes that might see them at the front of the house. Daniel got out his guitar and played some of his new songs, stopping now and then to change a word or alter a chord. Ben and Max were due back from honeymoon in a few days. Daniel resolved to call Ben's assistant in the morning to schedule some studio time. The sooner he got these songs recorded, the sooner he could present them to his record label. He'd decided that was what he wanted to do.

It would be a hard sell. The label was keen for him to record a new batch of covers for his next release, or a Christmas album. That was the last thing he wanted. Maybe they could reach a compromise. If they let him release the new stuff this year, he'd deliver the Christmas covers next year.

And if they turned him down, he'd walk away. He'd already completed his four-album deal. Each release going forward was negotiated on a record-by-record basis. He could find another label or go it alone. Why not? Plenty of artists released their own music these days. He wouldn't even need a distribution deal. He could sell the album through his website and at his shows. When these songs were recorded, he wanted to tour and perform them live. The road was already calling to him.

Around nine thirty, Daniel realized he was exhausted. The flight from Corfu had taken only four hours, but he found flying a tiring experience. The waiting around, the hustle of the airport, followed by the pure boredom of the flight itself. He'd rather travel by sea, no matter how much longer it took.

"How about an early night?" he asked Elijah.

Elijah closed the book he'd been reading, a huge tome on European cooking. He took off his glasses and squeezed the bridge of his nose. "Good idea. I've read the same paragraph three times and I'm done in."

Upstairs, while he waited for Elijah to brush his teeth, Daniel glanced out of the bedroom window. The street beyond their gates was empty. The press and fans had all left. Thank God. It was like living in a zoo when they were out there. He closed the blinds and the curtains, shutting out the night for good.

Elijah came out of the bedroom in just his white underwear. His suntan skin looked even more remarkable in the everyday environment of their bedroom. Daniel brushed his hand across Elijah's torso as he passed.

"Looking good, Mr. Mann," he said, copping a cheeky feel of his butt.

Elijah batted his hand away with a smile. "You're insatiable."

"Only for you. You're just too damned sexy."

"Can you wait until morning? Tonight, I'm too damned tired."

In truth, they both were. Daniel was content to slip naked beneath the covers and spoon in the warm curve of Elijah's spine. The comfort of their bed was familiar and assuring. Daniel fell asleep within minutes of turning out the light.

* * * *

His eyes opened suddenly an hour later, alert to a change within the house.

Something had woken him. A sound. What was it? He lay still, waiting for it to come again.

His mind raced through the options. He lay curled against Elijah. He would have to roll over to reach the baseball bat he had secreted beneath the bed.

The noise came again. The creak of a floorboard. Close. Very close.

Inside the room.

As his eyes came into focus, he saw the broad silhouette of a figure, standing at the foot of the bed.

Chapter Five

Daniel kept still and prayed the intruder could not see the whiteness of his eyes in the dark. The slow, rhythmic breath on the pillow beside him told him Elijah was still asleep.

He stared at the figure. Just a large shape in the darkness. Indistinct and broad. They might have a hood over their head.

How had they gotten in? Why hadn't they triggered the alarm?

The answer to those questions could wait till later. If they survived.

No doubt about that. No fucking way. After all they'd gone through, they weren't about to be slaughtered in their bed now. Whoever the intruder was, they'd made a big mistake, and they would pay dearly for it.

Their breath was quick and rasping in the dark. As his sight improved, Daniel saw something in their hand, pointed toward the bed. Then he noticed a tiny red light. It was a camera or a phone. The bastard was filming them.

Enough was enough. His jaw tightened as he fought to keep his fury in check. He had one shot at this. One chance to take them by surprise. A second or two at best. The intruder thought he was asleep. When he made his move, it would have to be fast.

He had a Taser in the top drawer and a baseball bat under the bed. Which was closer? The Taser, he reckoned. He could reach it without much difficulty. And if he struck a body blow, it would buy him enough time to reach the bat.

The intruder was still filming. No sign of any weapon. Not that he could see well enough in this light. The thick jacket they wore could conceal a knife, a gun, a rope. Anything. They could not be allowed to use them.

Thankfully, Daniel's right hand was beneath his pillow and not trapped under Elijah. He could do this. He knew the room well enough to find his way in the dark. Unlike the intruder. That was one advantage he had over them.

Slowly, quietly, he took a deep breath then sprang like a cat. He rolled across the bed and yanked open the drawer with his right hand. The Taser was the size and shape of a slim torch. He grabbed it as he threw back the covers and leapt from the bed.

The intruder let out a grunt. They turned and rushed for the door. Naked, Daniel went after them. He didn't care they were running away. They'd had the balls to break into his house and film him while he slept. They deserved everything they had coming to them.

There was another thud as the intruder misjudged the exit and banged into the chest of drawers. Daniel took full advantage of the delay and grabbed the back of their jacket, pulling down the hood. The Taser wouldn't work through the padding of their coat, so he moved quickly, ramming the weapon into the small of their neck, and discharged the five-second bolt of electricity. The intruder dropped to the floor, hitting their head on the oak drawers as they went down.

"What the hell?" Elijah sat up in bed and turned on his side lamp. Dazed, he shielded his eyes against the sudden glare. "What's going on?"

Daniel gasped for breath.

Looking at the figure on the floor, he recognized the red padded jacket and the shoulder-length auburn hair.

It was Lauren Warwick.

Stupefied, she clutched her mobile phone in her fleshy hand.

"What? What's she doing here?" Elijah asked, his voice still thick with sleep.

"She broke in," Daniel said numbly. Now his adrenaline levels had dropped and his limbs trembled.

"Shit, Daniel, what did you do? Is she dead?"

Why does he care about her? In that moment, Daniel wouldn't have minded if he had killed her. The fury her intrusion had triggered consumed him.

Elijah fell to his knees beside the still body. He grabbed her wrist and felt for a pulse, looking at Daniel with wide, concerned eyes, before relaxing.

"She hit her head on the way down," Daniel explained without feeling.

Elijah examined her skull with the tips of his fingers. "There's no blood. I think she's okay, but you'd better call an ambulance."

"Fuck that," Daniel said, pulling on his underpants. "I'm calling the police. I want the bitch arrested. She broke into our home. Our bedroom, for fuck's sake. Check her pockets for knives before she comes around."

Daniel grabbed his phone and dialed the emergency number while he hurried along the hall to his study. The Taser was a prohibited weapon in this country. Illegal for a member of the public to own or even attempt to buy one. Crazy that they couldn't be used for self-defense in such a dangerously fucked-up world, but he wasn't about to face criminal charges for protecting himself. He locked it in his office safe.

When he returned to the bedroom, Elijah had put on shorts and a T-shirt and sat on the edge of the bed with Lauren, who was fully awake. She held the side of her head where she'd fallen. She had a bath towel draped across her damp crotch. She must have wet herself when the Taser discharged. He looked quickly at her neck and could see no mark left by the device.

If she told the cops he'd stunned her, he would deny it, as simple as that.

"The police are on their way," he said.

"Oh, man," Lauren groaned. "You don't need to tell the pigs. Just let me go and I won't bother you no more. I give you my word."

"Your word isn't worth shit," Daniel said angrily. "You camp on my doorstep and break into my house. You're going to face the police all right. And if I have my way, you'll be going to jail for as many years as they can pin on you."

"Daniel," Elijah said. "Ease up."

Daniel glared at him furiously. *Whose side is he on?*

"Yeah," Lauren said with a sly smile. "Ease up, Daniel. I was on my way out when you assaulted me." Her eyes shone with hope as she plotted her escape. "You're not meant to attack someone if they're leaving. Even if they shouldn't be there in the first place. You could get into trouble. Maybe you're the one who'll go to jail."

"Nice try," he said. The stupid cow didn't realize she'd been shocked. That was something. "But you fell and hit your head when you were running away. An accident. You knocked yourself out. And your website is evidence of your obsession with me. You've been stalking us for months. Half a dozen witnesses saw you outside the house this afternoon. I dare bet those reporters have even got photos of you. I think my version of the story carries more credibility than yours."

She tutted and stuck out her bottom lip. "I used to think you were such a nice guy."

"I was, Lauren, believe me. Until I attracted the attention of crazies like you."

* * * *

The police arrived and took her away. A constable called Teaman stayed behind to take statements from Daniel and Elijah. CCTV footage of the grounds showed Lauren scaling the wall and approaching the house from the rear garden. She'd piled up the patio furniture to gain entry through one of the upstairs windows.

"Why didn't the alarm go off?" Daniel asked as he watched the footage. *Unbelievable.*

Elijah shook his head. "She came in upstairs. Only the downstairs windows have sensors. The security people said it wasn't necessary with all the other protection we have."

"You have got to be joking." He couldn't believe what he was hearing. How could Elijah have been so lax?

"Protection? Look how easily that fuckwit got in. A kid with a camera phone. What if it wasn't her? What if it was someone who meant serious business? Another Sonny Rock. They could have slit our throats while we slept. This house has no protection at all."

"It's very unusual for an intruder to attempt entry while the owners are home," PC Teaman said. The tone of his voice, aimed to calm Daniel down, only irritated him more.

"And yet this one did. We've been away for six weeks and she breaks in the night we return. We've had two attempts on our lives in two years. Fuck me. Why isn't anyone taking this seriously?"

"We take matters like this very seriously, Mr. Blake," PC Teaman said. "Lauren has already admitted gaining entry. The chances are we'll have her in front of the court tomorrow."

Daniel sighed. They didn't get it. Lauren Warwick was an idiot kid with an unhealthy obsession. A pest for sure, but she wasn't the real problem. Getting in as effortlessly as she had proved they were wide open to a more determined attack. They might as well have left the doors unlocked.

He could almost understand the police's antipathy to the situation, but why had Elijah been so sloppy? He should have insisted every window in the house was alarmed. And to act as if Daniel were in the wrong for Tasering the bitch. Had he lost all bloody sense?

Daniel headed for the stairs.

"Where are you going?" Elijah called after him.

"To pack," he barked. "I'm not spending another night in this house. We should never have come back."

Chapter Six

Early on Thursday morning, Elijah walked Daniel the five minutes from their hotel to the train station. They had spent the last two nights in a suite at the city center Hilton.

"I don't need a chaperone," Daniel said testily when Elijah pulled on his jacket to accompany him.

Though they were speaking to each other, their relationship remained strained. Elijah knew they were too strong-willed to back down, either of them. Daniel could have killed that girl with his Taser. God knows where he got the damn thing. Did he even know the power of its discharge? Suppose the girl had an underlying heart defect. One blast and she'd have been dead on their floor. Elijah was just as angry with himself. He'd known all about Daniel's secret weapons stash and had turned a blind eye to it, never expecting him to use them.

The alarm fiasco was also his fault. Shouldn't have listened to the security guy who said upstairs sensors were unnecessary, that intruders never came in through the upper level. Maybe that was true of opportunistic burglars, but not the kind of lunatics they'd drawn attention from. Elijah had fucked up.

Big time.

At the train station, he walked Daniel to the ticket barrier. They both wore peaked caps pulled low over their foreheads and glasses, trying to avoid attention. It had worked so far. The hotel staff had let them out of a side door to avoid the press gang at the main entrance.

Daniel was about to go through the barrier when Elijah grabbed his hand. He couldn't let him go like this. It would be wrong to part on sour terms.

"I am sorry," he said. He'd apologized a dozen times already but had never meant it more than this. "I made a mistake with the alarm. A huge mistake. If the whole house was covered, Lauren wouldn't have made it as far as she did."

Daniel stared at him. His mouth was a straight, emotionless line, but Elijah noted a softening in the tension around his eyes.

"I don't want to fight," Daniel said at last. "We're not one of those couples who thrive on angst and arguments."

"I agree. I hate the tension between us. I'll put it right. The new security system will be finished today. I'm going back to the house to check on progress this morning. More sensors, more cameras, they're even putting locks on the bedroom doors. It'll never happen again."

Daniel shook his head. "I meant what I said the other night. I'm not going back there. It's tainted. We'll speak to an estate agent this weekend. I want to put the house up to let and find a new place to live."

"Lauren can't come back," Elijah said softly.

"I'm not worried about her. She only wanted to film some crazy footage. But she got in with such minimal effort. Another Sonny would get to us with no trouble."

"Someone like that could get us anywhere."

Daniel sighed. "And that's exactly why I won't apologize for my Taser. If someone does come after us, we need every advantage we can get. I won't think twice about using it." He patted the side of his leather satchel. "And I'm not going anywhere without it again. If you go back to the house, you'll find another with a charger in the bottom drawer of my desk. Take it. Carry it with you."

Now Elijah sighed. "No. I've got a can of mace and a personal alarm, but I draw the line at that thing."

He'd already had to lie in his statement to the police, backing up Daniel's version of events, that Lauren knocked herself out when she hit her head on the dresser trying to escape. Thankfully, she'd pleaded guilty to the offense when she appeared before the court yesterday. If she hadn't, and the case had gone to trial, he'd have had to perjure himself in the witness box. They both would have. Making them no better than any other criminal.

An announcement came over the tannoy — Daniel's train was approaching the platform.

"I have to go."

Elijah pulled him into a tight embrace. None of this was worth the pain of them not getting along. "Take care," he said. "And be careful."

"Always," Daniel said, kissing him on the mouth. The kiss was soft, almost forgiving. "And you."

"What time will you be home tonight?"

"I'm not sure. Probably late. It depends how much Rachel wants to talk and what she has to say." He broke apart and slid his ticket into the machine to step through the barrier. "But, Elijah, I'll return to the hotel tonight, not the house."

Elijah nodded solemnly. "I'll see you there."

* * * *

In the last year Daniel had discovered he had a previously unknown talent for accents. He could often hear a voice and replicate the dialect in every way. It had proved to be a great distraction while killing time on the London run of *Lady Lynda*, where he would mimic the crew members and fans he met at the stage door.

Now he'd found a good use for the ability.

He went unnoticed for most of the train journey apart from the woman who brought the refreshment trolley through the carriage.

"Oh my God," she exclaimed, drawing a flurry of attention from the other first-class passengers. "You're him, aren't you? It's you?"

Without a beat, Daniel replied in a strong Scottish accent, South Lothian to be exact. "No, I'm just told I look like him. Happens all the time."

"Oh," she said, her smile wavering. "You're, well, the spitting image. You look just like him."

"Can't see it myself," he continued, "but plenty of people say so." He'd been wise enough to keep the baseball cap and glasses on for the duration of the journey, looking nothing like his usual image.

She gave him a coffee and moved on. He was aware of her glancing back at him as she advanced through the carriage, but he avoided eye contact again.

He'd checked the online editions of several newspapers during the trip and knew that he featured in most of them. The break-in on Tuesday had provided fodder for most of the tabloids. An intruder gaining entry to the house on their first night home highlighted the unreliability of their security. Most of the papers ran photos of their return earlier in the day.

More interesting were the features they wrote about Lauren Warwick. If he'd done his own research when she had first taken an interest in him, none of it would have come as a surprise. Lauren had form for celebrity stalking, both online and in person. A well-known social media troll, she had accounts in several names, running hate campaigns as well as fan pages, often on the same celebrity. She had once been arrested at Manchester Arena when she had tried to get backstage at a Kylie Minogue concert. And again at the Savoy Theatre in London, when an actress had returned to her dressing room during the interval of the show and found Lauren in her makeup chair, trying on wigs.

The girl had been regarded as an irritant rather than any real danger to the people she fixated on, though a breakfast news presenter had taken out a restraining order against her after she'd sent a series of malicious letters to the studio.

Now she was in prison. For the next few weeks at least. After her guilty plea at the magistrate's court yesterday, her case had been committed to crown court three weeks from now, where the judge would have more authority to hand out a serious sentence. Whatever happened to her, Daniel had already instructed his lawyer to apply for a restraining order. He didn't want her coming anywhere near him or Elijah again.

The train arrived into King's Cross Station midmorning.

Daniel drew a handful of curious glances but made it out of the station without being stopped. He jumped into a cab and gave the driver instructions using the Scottish accent and caught his questioning glance in the rearview mirror before pulling away.

Traffic around King's Cross is heavy at any time of day and this was no exception. He sat in the back and gazed at the familiar streets, thronged with cabs, buses, bikes and cars. During his run at the Palladium, he used to go home every Saturday night to spend his day off in Leeds. A driver would take him from the theater to his front door, but he always caught the train back on Monday afternoon ahead of the evening show. He'd become so used to seeing ads for *Lady Lynda* across the city and on the sides of buses, plastered with smiling images of himself and Max, it was a shock to see the same ads today promoting their replacements. The show continued to be a massive hit. He'd heard that while business had taken a slight dip following the recast, it still played to full houses and standing ovations every weekend.

Good thing too. The show deserved to run for years and he hoped it would.

The cab arrived at the Waldorf Hotel in Aldwych. Daniel paid and tipped the driver before hurrying through the door with his head dipped low. Once inside, he turned right, passing through the lobby to the stylish, wood-paneled bar. He scanned the handful of people who were there—no sign of Keeley—before choosing a table behind the door, away from the windows.

This was not a day to be seen.

A waiter came to take his order. Keeping up the Scottish accent, he ordered tea for two people and a sharing platter of sandwiches.

Keeley Rank walked through the door, just as the waiter left.

"Over here," he called in his Scottish brogue.

Keeley turned, her expression surprised, before she realized who he was and came over. "What's with the voice?" she asked, sliding into the opposite seat.

"Trying to go unnoticed," he murmured.

"Is it working?"

"Holding up so far."

Keeley went nowhere incognito. Her trademark blonde hair was whiter than ever, save for a good half-inch of black roots. Her makeup was heavy and overstated. She had opted to wear a severe navy suit and silk blouse that would have looked businesslike if she hadn't teamed it with an abundance of costume jewelry. "I'm loving today's headlines," she said dryly. "You sure know how to attract the weirdos. What is it about you? Pheromones or something?"

"If I knew what it was, I would stop it."

Keeley grinned. "That Lauren girl is a complete idiot. She tried trolling me a few months back. Dumb bitch. I practically invented internet-cuntiness. I don't know how she thought she'd get one over on me. By the time I shared her pathetic attempts with two million of my toxic followers she soon made off with her tail between her legs."

"Why do you encourage them?" Daniel asked, staring at her. "Can't you ignore them?"

"Of course I could. But where would the fun be in that? I like to wind them up and watch them go. Silly little fuckwits."

Daniel shook his head. He would never understand Keeley's attitude. She lived to antagonize people. Elijah once said she could start an argument in an empty room. Daniel didn't doubt it.

The tea arrived with the platter of sandwiches. Daniel set about pouring while Keeley opened her enormous handbag and pulled out a batch of manila folders. When it came to writing, Keeley was old school, preferring to show him hard copies of the various drafts rather than email them. Daniel's theory was that she didn't trust him with an electronic version. That she was scared he might change something.

"I finished the chapter on Sonny's back story," she said, handing him a file. "Nothing we didn't already know, but check it out. I've added quotes from a couple of old cell mates and expanded the part about his ex-wife. She still won't talk to me but I got a handle on their marriage from a woman who used to live upstairs from them. She had plenty to say. Most of it was pure speculation but I've used what I could corroborate."

"I'll read it on the train home," he said, putting the folder aside. "What time is Rachel coming?"

"Two. I wanted to have the chance to talk first." She put another folder on the table between them. "Take a look."

Daniel opened it. There were several typed pages together with a bunch of photocopied pictures. They were school photos, group shots of kids around twelve years old. "What's this?"

"Gold is what is it." She sipped her tea. "Transcripts of an interview I did with two people who were at school with Oliver. They knew him pretty well from about nine through to sixteen. As well as anyone knew him, that is. Oliver was a loner, even then, with something of a temper. This kid's anger issues were off the scale. He had a chip on his shoulder the size of this hotel. Bigger."

"That figures." Daniel looked at the photographs. Despite the passage of over twenty years, he had no trouble picking Oliver from the class of awkward-looking kids. He would recognize that sharp, unsmiling face anywhere. Oliver gazed with contempt and distain from the back row of the group, looking pissed off that he had to share the moment with thirty other kids.

"So, it was common knowledge among the school that Oliver was adopted," Keeley said, "and kids being the nasty little bastards that they are, they tormented him. Mercilessly."

"Why didn't they keep it quiet till he was older?"

"They couldn't. With his birth mother dumping him in the doorway of a hospital when he was born, it was big news. When Rhonda Gill adopted him, she made a big show of it. Local news and all that shit. It was never a secret. The people I spoke to freely admit to bullying him. They're sorry about it now, but too late. They tormented him at the time. All the kids did."

Daniel turned the page and found another photo taken a few years later when Oliver was around fourteen and had bleached his hair to his more familiar look.

"As he got older, they say his behavior worsened," Keeley continued. "He fought back against the bullies and was once suspended for attacking another boy in the gym. They left him alone after that. Nobody picked on him, but no one was in a rush to befriend him either. He was very much a loner."

Daniel looked at the blank eyes of the boy in the picture, so empty, so lost. He'd had plenty of friends himself at that age, joining after-school groups and amateur theater. He wondered how he'd have handled Oliver if he'd known him at the time. No better than anyone else, he guessed. Sure, kids could be cruel, but they didn't have the skills to deal with difficult situations or personalities. He could never have been friends with him. They were too different. He wouldn't understand the darkness, the pain and anger at the heart of a boy like Oliver.

"It's sad," he said, looking through the pictures again.

"Don't go misty-eyed on me." Keeley took a sandwich and nibbled the corner. "That's the face of a killer you're looking at. And from everyone I've talked to, it's obvious he had a very tenuous grip on reality way back then."

"That doesn't make it right," Daniel said. "He was let down. By school, family, doctors — hell, someone must have read the signs. If they got him the help he needed as a teenager, he could have lived a normal life. Somebody should have done something."

Keeley swallowed and dabbed her mouth with a napkin. "That's a question we can put to his sister when she gets here. You may be right, but I think he'd have ended up in trouble, regardless." She produced another photograph. Oliver, this time around twenty-five, pictured with another young man. It was a selfie in front of a promenade. "Manny Brogan. They went out for just over a year. They even moved in together. But not for long. Oliver was insanely jealous if Manny even spoke to another man. I talked to Manny a few weeks ago, and he described a relationship that ticked every box for controlling, domestic-violence behavior. Oliver alienated Manny from his friends and family, harassed him at work and was violent toward him if he didn't get his own way. What you could call a prize prick."

Daniel sighed, looking at the photo again. Wherever Oliver went, he left a trail of emotional damage in his wake. "What happened?"

"Obviously they broke up," Keeley said. "But it was far from pretty. Oliver harassed Manny for a long time afterward. It was a typical, far from reasoned response. He trashed Manny's flat, tore up his clothes, damaged his car, sent personal pictures to his family and place of work. Grade A arsehole behavior from the man we've come to know so well."

Know so well. Is that even true? Oliver Gill remained unknowable, however much they discovered. He was an enemy too complex and deep to ever know completely. He wondered if Rachel would have any of the answers.

"What do you think about his sister?" he asked.

"I've only spoken to her on the phone. Briefly at that. She's scared too. It hasn't been easy. Poor cow. People have taken it out on her for what her brother did. The abuse has been excessive. I can take what people say to me and give it right back to them, but Rachel isn't like that. She took a lot of the sour shit personally. It was personal, I suppose. She moved house a couple of times. Pulled the kids out of school."

"Shit," Daniel said. "All because of her brother?"

"Oliver's actions have had a far-reaching ripple effect."

Daniel nodded. "What made her change her mind? She's refused all your requests for an interview in the past. Why agree to it now?"

"An opportunity to put her side across. I promised her there'd be no bias or agenda. I'll write her story exactly as she tells it. Even if it's at odds with the rest of the book."

"That's fair enough," Daniel said. He didn't blame Oliver's sister for what he'd done, though he'd been suspicious of her in the aftermath of the Blackpool attack, and wondered if she might have been pulling Sonny's strings. The police found no evidence to connect the two. If anything, her own experiences got worse in the aftermath.

Keeley's phone rang. "It's her," she said, glancing at the display. She hurried to take the call away from any keen eavesdroppers. Daniel glanced back through the folder she'd given him, looking at the photos, reading the transcripts of interviews. He had to give Keeley her due, she had been as thorough and far-reaching in her commitment to the book as she'd promised.

Their collaboration hadn't been easy. She started the process by taking his own account. They spent two weeks together last December, going through his story, looking at Overload and his earlier encounters with Oliver, recounting every minute of those three days onboard the *Anthem*. It was an uncomfortable experience but they could never have got to the heart of the story without his own commitment.

But here they were, all this time later, huge files of evidence gathered, and no nearer to finding out who had hired Sonny than at the start.

Daniel took a sandwich from the platter—cream cheese and cucumber on tomato bread—but found it difficult to swallow. Frustration constricted his throat.

When Keeley returned, her face was like thunder. Daniel knew what she was going to say before she spoke.

"She's not coming," Keeley snapped, sitting back down and slamming her fist on the table. "This morning's headlines about your latest stalker have panicked her. She won't leave the house."

"Shit."

They'd come so close to learning something new. Now they had nothing.

Chapter Seven

"This place is locked up tighter than Fort Knox."

Elijah looked skeptically at the security guy and wondered whether they all followed the same script. "I've heard that before. Those exact words. So, excuse me if I take some convincing."

The engineer, a rotund figure in his late fifties, shook his head. "Nothing to worry about. If you'd come to us in the first place, you wouldn't have had a problem."

The entire alarm system had been replaced with sensors fitted to every door and window, upstairs and down. There were additional motion captor sensors throughout the house and extra CCTV cameras, both inside and out.

"A mouse couldn't get in without tripping an alarm," the man assured him.

Elijah took him at his word. The system appeared second to none. He hoped Daniel would be convinced but doubted it. When he had left this morning, he'd been adamant he wouldn't be back. Elijah hoped he'd change his mind, but if not, they would move on. Daniel was more important than any house.

When the engineer left, he went up to their bedroom to gather extra clothes and underwear. Verona had been in since their hurried exit and had straightened the place. She'd changed the bed, dealt with their holiday laundry and even cleaned the carpet where Lauren had wet herself. He packed enough clothes to last them a couple more days. He hoped he could convince Daniel to come back by the weekend. They were due to leave again next Monday, up to Durham, ahead of the gala dinner taking place there.

Shit. With everything else that had happened, he'd forgotten to complete the menu for dinner. With five hundred guests, April would be having a fit right now. He went back to the kitchen and found the book of notes he'd made over the summer.

There was no point stressing over this, not when they had bigger problems. He decided to use Kostas' kleftiko recipe for the main meat course. It was simplicity itself. He would put the lamb on the lowest heat at the start of the day and let it cook in a blend of herbs and its own juices till they were ready. He'd think of some fancy chef-y way to present it so the fine-dining punters didn't think they were being swindled.

As he searched his notes for a suitable vegetarian option, Daniel called to say he had to stay over in London.

"Rachel got cold feet and canceled," he explained, "but Keeley's talked her around. Only we're meeting tomorrow morning instead of today."

"Will you be okay?" Elijah asked. "You didn't pack an overnight bag."

"It's fine," Daniel said. "I got a room at the hotel here. I plan to spend the night reading through Keeley's notes and the latest chapters. There's a chemist round the corner in Covent Garden. I'll go out later to grab a few toiletries. I won't need much for one night. Will just have to go commando tomorrow, that's all."

Elijah laughed. "I can come down if you like. Bring you some fresh pants and stay over. It's not too late to catch a train."

"It's okay. I'll survive one night. Besides, you've got things to do yourself. How's it going?"

He told Daniel about the new security system. "I can't see it failing."

"That's what they said last time. You're not going to stay in the house tonight, are you?"

"I wasn't planning to, but then again, I thought you'd be coming home. I don't much fancy the hotel on my own. Besides, this place is probably more secure than anywhere."

Daniel groaned. "I'd feel better if you didn't."

"I know," he said softly. "But I can't live by fear."

"Can't you get your brother to stay the night?"

"Harry's working away at the minute. He's in Dublin, I think. I'll be fine on my own. I'm a big boy."

"No," Daniel said. "I'll come home. I'll catch an early train to London in the morning."

"You won't," Elijah asserted. "Stay where you are. I can take care of myself. I've got a ton of work to do. I'll lock all the doors, set the alarm and check in with you every hour if it'll make you happy, but we have to do this. Otherwise, we let the enemy defeat us and destroy our lives."

Reluctantly, Daniel agreed to stay in London. Elijah understood his concern, but he didn't agree with it.

They had to live as normal a life as possible. That didn't mean being stupid, or taking risks. They had to remain alert, but they couldn't go on in a state of constant fear. This house was probably the safest place in the world right now. Safer than any hotel. They'd been in a hotel when Sonny attacked them.

He was more worried about Daniel down in London on his own. But he had faith that the man he loved could look after himself. He'd be tooled up with Tasers and mace and things Elijah was better off not knowing about.

They had to get on with it.

Elijah had written out a menu for the first four of five courses when his phone sounded a text alert. It was from Joe Elliot.

Hi. On my way to Leeds and need a place to crash. Can you guys put me up?

Elijah laughed out loud. Daniel was a quick thinker. Joe wasn't due to arrive until Sunday night before traveling to Durham with them on Monday ahead of the dinner. Daniel must have called him soon after they got off the phone.

A thirty-five-year-old man with a twenty-one-year-old babysitter. *Nice one, Daniel.*

With a smile, Elijah texted straight back.

Of course we can. Let me know when your train gets in and I'll pick you up.

He wasn't angry, as daft as the idea was. It would be nice to have company this evening. He hadn't seen Joe for months. They had a lot to catch up on.

He finished his menu and emailed the details to April Evie, so she could place the order for ingredients. There were several unread messages from her in the inbox. They could wait. She had what she needed from him now. He powered down his laptop and went to make the spare room ready for Joe.

* * * *

On his way to the station, Elijah called at the Hilton to empty their suite and check out. Now he'd decided to go home, there was no point keeping it on. He didn't need that safety net. If Daniel refused to come to the house on his return, they would find somewhere else. Elijah hoped that wouldn't be the case.

As he turned the corner to the station, Joe was waiting outside with a small suitcase, smoking a cigarette. Each time Elijah saw him, he experienced a fresh stab of sadness. Joe Elliot was a shadow of the boy he'd been before the assault in Blackpool.

He glanced furtively at the car as Elijah pulled up beside him and, only when he realized who was driving, smiled.

Joe had always been a slender kid but had lost weight since Elijah had seen him last. The jeans and hoodie he wore looked two sizes too large. Like Daniel, he'd taken to wearing baseball caps in public, with the peak pulled low over his brow. Beneath the cap, Elijah noted the sharpness of his cheekbones.

This boy needs a few square meals.

Joe stubbed out his cigarette as Elijah got out of the car.

"So good to see you," Elijah said, throwing his arms around him. As they embraced, he realized just how thin Joe had become. It was like hugging a bag of bones. Elijah hid his concern.

Joe's smile was wide, familiar and reassuringly genuine. "You too. The holiday has done you good. You look incredible. The suntan suits you."

"Holiday? What holiday?" So much had happened since they'd come home, the six weeks in Greece were a distant memory. He lifted Joe's case into the boot of the car and they both climbed into the front. "Hey. Have you eaten? Are you hungry?"

Joe shook his head. "I had coffee on the train."

"I'm starving. C'mon, let's see if we can get a table at Browns. My treat. It's the least I can do for my babysitter."

Joe laughed. "I'm glad we don't have to pretend. I've been trying to think of an excuse the whole way here to explain my early arrival."

"Daniel could at least have given you that."

Joe took off the cap and ruffled his thick, dark blond hair. "You're not mad, are you?"

"Not a bit. I was looking forward to seeing you anyway. This way, we get to spend more time together."

He was grateful there was no awkwardness between him and Joe. The lad once had a serious crush on him but was over it. Now they were good friends. Elijah never asked what Joe was doing in Daniel's room, dressed in nothing but a jockstrap, the night Sonny tried to kill them. It didn't matter. Joe had saved their lives. If he hadn't been there, they would be dead.

But it was Joe himself who had revealed what he was doing. He'd wanted them to know before it came out in court. He'd stolen Daniel's key and let himself into the suite with a threesome in mind. He'd wept and hung his head in shame when he related his story.

They'd assured him it didn't matter. Not one bit. They didn't care why he was there or what he was doing. All that mattered were the actions he'd taken. Quick thinking and smart, he was a hero.

At the restaurant, Elijah asked the maître d' for a quiet table, away from the windows and the busy bar area. Joe looked uncomfortable and kept his cap on until they were seated out of sight.

"Good?" Elijah asked.

Joe nodded, cautious and tight-lipped. His olive-colored eyes flicked about the room.

A good-looking waiter came to the table with menus. "Hi, guys. Welcome to Browns. My name is Callum. I'll be serving you this evening."

Callum was in his mid-twenties, tall and slim, with short black hair and a friendly Geordie accent. Elijah noticed the way Joe's eyes widened as Callum took their order for drinks, and the surreptitious way he checked him out from his tight waist to the handsome smile.

"Cute, eh?" Elijah said when Callum disappeared.

Joe reddened. "He's all right," he said, burying his face in the menu. "What do you recommend here?"

Elijah didn't push it. He'd love to see Joe come out of his shell a little and recapture something of the boy he used to be. As far as he knew, Joe hadn't had a boyfriend since Blackpool, and still lived at home with his mother. Elijah couldn't blame him. The world had proven to be a scary place.

When Daniel was starring in *Lady Lynda*, he staged a one-off solo concert at the Royal Albert Hall. Though he didn't publicize the fact, he gave all the proceeds from the night to Joe. It was a life-changing amount of money for a man his age. Enough to quit his job, buy a house, start a new life. As of now, he had done none of those things. He still worked as a backstage dresser at the Winter Gardens.

At least that was something. A lot of people would have hidden away with a sick note from their doctor. Elijah hoped the job would eventually give him back his confidence.

They all dealt with the ordeal in their own ways. For him, it was a change of career, for Daniel it was baseball bats and mace, and for Joe it was carrying on just like before.

Except nothing was like before.

"Are you looking forward to the gala?" Elijah asked brightly, trying to change the subject.

"Uh-huh," Joe said, still looking at the menu.

"You don't sound it."

"I am," he said, taking his time to look up. "Just nervous, I guess. I'm not used to formal events. I've had to hire a suit. I'll feel like a fish out of water."

"You won't be on your own. Daniel and Max will be on the stage, but you're sitting with Ben. You get on all right with him, don't you? And as soon as I'm finished in the kitchen, I'll join you at the table. It'll be fun."

Joe nodded, unsmiling. "I know. It's just that, well, I kind of…haven't been out since the wrap party for *Lady Lynda*."

Elijah looked at him incredulously. "You haven't been out at all?"

"I have. Just not to anything like this. A big event, I mean. I've gone for drinks a few times with the guys at work, and for dinner, but nothing more."

It was worse than Elijah thought. If Joe wasn't careful, he'd become a hermit. It had almost happened to Daniel in the aftermath of the *Anthem*. He hid himself away and didn't want to go out, didn't want to see anyone, didn't want to work.

Ultimately work had been his salvation. Maybe Joe just needed a similar incentive.

Incentive of another kind came moments later when Callum returned with their drinks and to take their order. Elijah couldn't miss the way they looked at each other throughout. For Joe, it was a series of shy, hesitant glances. For Callum, things were much more obvious. With wide eyes and an even wider smile, he flirted full-on.

"He's nice, don't you think?" Elijah said when they were alone again.

Joe gave a small nod of confirmation.

"I think he's into you," Elijah encouraged.

Joe's eyes opened, full of hope, but he said, "I doubt it. I don't think so. He's out of my league."

"What? Are you mad? He's perfect for you. Didn't you see the way he looked at you?"

"He was just being friendly. That's what they pay him for. He's probably straight."

"You need to get your gaydar checked. He's definitely not straight, and he definitely does fancy you."

Joe gave the first joyous and genuine smile Elijah had seen since his arrival. It looked good and made him look his own age rather than several years older.

"Give it a rest." He laughed. "Let's talk about something else. Like why you need a minder tonight."

Elijah groaned. "Let's not talk about that."

The meal was agreeable. Elijah kept the mood and conversation light though he couldn't stop watching Joe as they ate. He played with his food, moving things about the plate, picking rather than eating with any appetite. It was heartbreaking to see a twenty-one-year-old with so little passion for life.

Callum made frequent returns to their table, checking they were okay more than any regular waiter, and each time he came by, Joe visibly brightened.

After the main course, Joe went outside for a cigarette, just before Callum came back to clear the table. Bad timing.

"Worked here long?" Elijah asked him.

"Just three weeks," he said. "Only two nights a week while I'm in uni."

"Ah. I wondered what a Geordie boy was doing in Leeds."

"You'd be surprised. We get everywhere," Callum joked. "What happened to your friend?"

"He'll be back in a minute." Elijah caught the way Callum looked hopefully toward the door. *Oh, what the hell. These two are gagging for each other.* "Don't tell him I said anything, but he likes you."

Callum's eyebrows shot up. "Really?"

"Really. He's a lovely lad but very shy. He would never say anything himself."

Callum pursed his lips thoughtfully as he collected their plates. And then he said, "So, if I asked him out, would he be too shy to say yes?"

"He might still be shy, but I think he'd like that. A lot."

Elijah smiled. Joe might not agree, but sometimes people needed a push in the right direction.

Chapter Eight

By morning, word had gotten around London journalists that Daniel had spent the night at the Waldorf, and a large group of photographers stood on the pavement outside the main entrance, waiting for their shot. Keeley, suspecting this might happen, had arranged to meet Rachel Gill at another location. Now Daniel had the problem of getting out of the hotel unnoticed and joining them without a crowd of paparazzi on his tail.

It would take more than a baseball cap and a Scottish accent to fool them today, but he'd had the foresight to bring another of his disguises. A curly black Poldark-style wig. He checked out at reception and persuaded hotel staff to let him exit through the kitchen. The disguise wouldn't hold up to scrutiny from the mob out front, but he counted on the back doors being less covered.

The gambit paid off. A kitchen assistant, stepping outside on the pretext of a smoke, informed him that there were four photographers in the back alley.

Those odds were a lot better.

Before the incredulous eyes of the staff, he changed his appearance in an instant. It was more than the wig. By altering his posture, his spine, his shoulders, the entire way he carried himself, he shrunk several inches. With a slight hunch of one shoulder and an angle of the head, he looked older and battered. If he could keep his distance from the photographers, he knew he would get away with it.

Stepping outside, he clocked the location of each cameraman. They'd split into two pairs, trying to cover the rear exits of the hotel. They sprang to attention as he approached.

Keep it together. It's a performance. Don't lose character.

With a short, slightly stiff gait, he crossed the road and set off toward Covent Garden. He was aware of their eyes on him the whole time. One of them fired off a few shots for security. Just in case. No one really thought it was him.

Daniel turned the corner onto Drury Lane. No one followed. He passed in front of the Theatre Royal, maintaining the same careful pace. All the way through Covent Garden, no one paid him any attention. Secretly pleased, he contained his smile. He was getting good at this. A far better actor than he ever got credit for.

They could keep the glory if it meant walking around in public unnoticed. As he approached the Seven Dials area, he stepped into a recessed doorway and, in a couple of deft moves, swapped the wig for the baseball cap. When he resumed his course, he'd altered his entire posture and pace. Risking a glance behind, he was pleased to note there was no one tailing him.

He caught a cab outside the Cambridge Theatre and gave the driver the address Keeley had provided on the other side of the river. It was a lawyer's office in Southwark. Keeley was waiting at the door when he arrived.

"Is she here?" he asked, hurrying inside before anyone on the street recognized him.

"Yep. I took her straight in before she got cold feet again."

"Is she all right? Will she talk to us?"

"I think so. Yesterday's headlines panicked her. You're rarely in the papers without her brother's name getting a mention. The poor cows had enough, that's all."

The interior of the office was very modern and corporate-looking, all stainless steel and glass with expensive art prints on the walls.

"What is this place?" Daniel asked.

"Just a poncy city law firm," she said none too quietly, leading him along a harshly lit corridor. "One of the senior partners owes me a big favor. His bratty son got a little rough with a couple of hookers at a friend's birthday bash last year. A sweet-sixteenth birthday. I took the story to Daddy rather than publish it. The girls got a generous payoff and I got free legal advice for life. He's letting me use one of the rooms today. At least it's private."

Once again, Daniel considered himself lucky to have Keeley Rank working for rather than against him.

She led him to a meeting room at the back of the building. Rachel Gill sat alone on the near side of a large conference table and looked up, startled, when they entered. She put down the phone she'd been looking at.

"Hello," Daniel said warmly, going straight to her with his hand extended. She looked terrified as she raised her own hand. He took it in a gentle hold. "Thanks so much for coming."

He had to assure her he had no animosity toward her.

She wasn't at all how he imagined. Though he knew well enough that Rachel and Oliver were not blood relatives, for some reason he'd imagined there'd be a family resemblance. There was none. Rachel was a petite woman in her mid-thirties. She had an attractive, plump face with warm brown eyes, and her auburn hair was cut into a short, pixie style. She wore jeans, flat shoes and a short, waist-length jacket.

"Hello," she said, looking away quickly. Tension was evident in her tight body language and, as she withdrew her hand, Daniel noticed how much it trembled.

"I do appreciate your coming," he reiterated. "We both do. And I'm sorry for the burden all this has placed on you."

She sat and, looking at the hands folded on her lap, said, "Every time you're in the papers, it starts again. Only yesterday some kids shouted at me in the street, and I get dirty looks every time I go to the shops. I try to do all the shopping online now. It's easier than going out and facing people. The last time I went to the supermarket, some woman followed me around, telling me what a horrible person I must be, from such an awful family."

"Shit," Daniel said, sitting opposite her. "I'm sorry. No one should have to go through that."

Her mouth turned downward. "They shouldn't have to, no, but I do. I don't know why I agreed to this interview. I don't see how your book will make things better. Part of me hopes that telling the full story will satisfy people's morbid curiosity. But then again, what good will it do? Those that behave the worst won't even read your book. They'll read a headline, or a tweet, or a Facebook post, and that's as deep as they'll go. That's as much as they need to condemn someone for life."

"We sincerely hope that won't be the case." Daniel couldn't promise her otherwise. She was right. The majority of people didn't want to know the truth. They had more fun sharing headlines and half-formed opinions about it all.

"We might not satisfy the hordes," Keeley said, opening a large note book, "but we'll get some of the answers we're looking for. If nothing else comes of this book, I'd like you, Daniel and everyone else involved to gain some personal peace from it."

"Peace," Rachel said, looking up. Her eyes were wet. "My husband left when it first came out. Our relationship wasn't good to begin with, but he couldn't cope with the attention we were under. So he walked, but not before taking a check for ten grand from the papers to tell the story of my brother. I haven't seen him since. Neither have our three kids. And if that wasn't enough, I've had to move to a new house twice and change their schools each time. They've all been bullied and have nightmares about their evil Uncle Oliver. So, excuse me if I can't grasp the concept of your book bringing any peace to my life."

Her words hung heavily in the silence that followed. Daniel could think of nothing to say that would comfort her. She was as much a victim of Oliver's actions as anyone. The damage might not be physical like it had been for the rest of them, but the emotional scars were just as pronounced.

"Anyway," Rachel said, pulling back her shoulders and sitting straight. "Can we just get on with this? I'd rather get it over and done with."

Keeley started recording. "Tell us your story."

Rachel's account covered much of what they already knew. Oliver had been found on the doorstep of an old folks' care home when he'd been just a few hours old. Despite an extensive search and mass media interest, his birth mother had never been located.

"It was always assumed she must have been a very young girl," Rachel said, taking a plastic folder from her bag and showing them clippings from local papers about the baby on the doorstep. "My mother kept a scrapbook of all this stuff. She believed the girl would come looking for her baby someday once she was older and regretted her decision. It didn't happen. Whoever that woman was, she had no interest in claiming the baby. The *Blackpool Gazette* used to revisit the story every few years while he was growing up. She had every opportunity to find him and didn't."

"Did Oliver want her to come for him?" Daniel asked.

Rachel shook her head. "Quite the opposite. He adored my mother. He used to say his birth mother did him a favor. Oliver and my mother were two of a kind. Showbusiness through and through. From a really young age he used to get in bed with her at the weekend and they'd paw through her celebrity magazines, or listen to music, singing along at the tops of their voices."

"Your mother was a singer?" Keeley asked.

"Semi-professional. She worked the club circuit in the North West for a few years, doing Tina Turner and Cher numbers. She had more confidence and volume than she did talent, but she got plenty of bookings.

That's how Oliver started too, singing round the local clubs. He was only sixteen when he began. I used to drive him and his equipment from venue to venue in my little Mini. Just like her, he had more confidence than talent, but it never held him back. And he got better with experience."

"This sounds like the two of you were close," Daniel said.

"We were. He was my little brother. I wanted to look after him."

"What did you think about him going up for the boy band?" Keeley asked.

"I was surprised at first. Oliver was never a team player, so being in a group didn't seem like a natural choice for him. He had his own look too. He wasn't model good-looking like most of those boy-band types. I couldn't see him fitting in, but Oliver was adamant he wanted to audition. I even went with him. We came to London for the day so he could attend the open call. Not for a moment did I think he would get it, but one call-back led to another, and before we knew it, he was part of Overload." Rachel poured herself some water from the jug on the table. She paused, seeming to gather her thoughts before continuing. "It was the biggest mistake he ever made. Oliver wasn't cut out for that kind of life. It went straight to his head. Before they'd even finished making their record, he told me how much better he was than the other boys. How he'd use them to get his first foot on the ladder of fame and then dump them. He used to call me up and tell me how he was going to be the next Robbie Williams, only bigger."

Daniel was familiar with the next part of the story. How Oliver's ego grew and his behavior deteriorated, leading to his dismissal from the band and, after a hasty audition process, Daniel taking his place.

"How did he handle the sacking?" he asked.

"Devastated," Rachel said. "Though he wouldn't show it, not even to me. It was a great act of bravado. He said he wasn't bothered, that he was better than Overload, that he was a solo artist. He tried to get a manager and record deal but no one would touch him. He blamed that guy who managed Overload – Sam, was it? He thought Sam had him blacklisted in the industry. He was mad when the first Overload record came out without him. He claimed he could still hear his own voice on the track. That all you did was sing over the top of him."

"No," Daniel said. "Oliver's vocals were taken off entirely. Sam was adamant about that. I re-recorded the whole album."

"Did Oliver express any violent ideas back then?" Keeley asked. "Did he ever talk about getting even? Or revenge?"

"God, no," Rachel said. "He wasn't like that. Not then. He was pissed off, for sure. Who wouldn't be? But he wouldn't have done anything to hurt you. He was too busy trying to build a career. In no time at all he was back working the club and cabaret scene, looking for another break. He was over the moon when the Overload album flopped and you were dropped by the label. He bought a bottle of champagne to celebrate that night. But that's as far as his animosity went."

Daniel took a deep breath. As pleased as he was to talk to Rachel, she hadn't told them anything they didn't already know. She went on, telling them about his second stab at fame, when he auditioned for the TV talent show *The One*, and his path crossed with Daniel's again.

"He was really pissed off after that, especially when you won, but again, I'm not aware of him harboring any dangerous thoughts. If anything, he was glad of the notoriety he gained when his episodes went out. It was a car crash to watch, but the phone started ringing afterward. He went on TV a few times to talk about it and his booking went up. He was able to charge more for gigs, for a while at least."

"What about relationships?" Keeley asked. "Was he seeing anyone significant at the time? Anyone who might have shared his animosity toward Daniel? Fueled it even?"

"No one. Oliver didn't really do boyfriends or relationships. I don't think anyone was ever good enough for him. He was also a self-professed slut. He was into hookup sites, sex parties and all that stuff. Quite proud of it at times. I never understood why. There were drugs and God knows what at those parties. Oliver promised me he was careful, but he would say that, wouldn't he?"

"So, you can't think of anyone who loved him well enough to avenge him now?" Keeley asked, her voice sharp.

"No."

"No?" Keeley's Botox-frozen forehead was immovable, but her voice was filled with incredulity. "Sonny Rock didn't hire himself, Rachel. Somebody paid him. Let's not forget he murdered two men, both fathers to young children, and he attempted to kill at least two more. Elijah Mann and Joe Elliott have life-changing injuries because of what he did. Someone hired him to do that. Someone who thought an awful lot of your brother."

Rachel's face turned an angry shade of red. "And you think that's me? Is that it? Do you think I want any of this? I've got three kids and no husband because of what we've been through. Broken windows and dog shit through my letterbox. Panic attacks every time I leave the house. I can't sleep for fear of what people might do to us in the night. Do you think I want that? No job and an ex-husband who won't pay maintenance. I haven't got a pot to piss in. Do you really think I've got a few thousand spare to hire a fucking hitman?"

* * * *

"You were hard on her at the end," Daniel said when they were alone.

"I had to get the bitch to crack," Keeley said. "That insipid sister act she put on got us nowhere."

"I thought she was very genuine," he said.

Keeley rolled her eyes as she packed up her recording equipment. "And that's why you'd never make it as a reporter. You have to question everyone and everything. And whatever they tell you, always assume they're lying until you prove otherwise."

"That's too cynical. Her life has been totally screwed up because of her brother. She's angry. We all are. You shouldn't have attacked her like that."

Rachel Gill had been reduced to tears by the end of the interview. Daniel had leapt to her defense as Keeley tore into her. It was obvious to him that Rachel had nothing to do with avenging Oliver's death. They would have to cast their nets even wider to find out who hired Sonny.

Keeley folded her arms on the table, leaned forward and gave him an eyeful of cleavage. "You believe her?"

"Yes," he said.

"All of it?"

"Pretty much. You heard her. About her kids, the bullying, the shit through the letterbox. Her life is hell. Why would she lie about it?"

Keeley looked at him and drummed her bejeweled fingers on the table. "And her husband running out on her. You believed that part too?"

"Yes."

"Well, part of her story is true. I know that without checking further. He did sell a story to the press."

"Again, she'd have no reason to lie about it. Check away. I'm sure she's telling the truth."

Keeley smiled, shaking her head. "Daniel, I said part of the story is true. He spoke to the papers all right, but he held out for a lot more than ten grand. The figure I heard was closer to thirty."

Daniel faltered. *Shit.* Why was he so willing to take people at face value? "Maybe he told Rachel ten so she wouldn't come after the money."

"And maybe he never really left. We only have her account of the separation. My next job is to speak to him, get his side. Because I have a hunch he spoke to the press on Rachel's orders."

He stared at her blankly as the possibility sank in.

"As for the hard-luck story," Keeley continued. "Well, I don't know what it costs to hire a man like Sonny to kill for you, but thirty thousand pounds will go a long way toward it. I'm sorry, Daniel, I can see you liked her, but Rachel Gill is still very much in the frame for wanting you dead."

Chapter Nine

Joe fidgeted in the passenger seat as Elijah steered the car through the early evening traffic. In a pair of slim-fitting jeans and a black T-shirt, it was obvious how much weight Joe had lost. His brown leather watch strap hung slack on his slender wrist as he drummed his fingers on his bony thighs.

"Try to relax," Elijah told him. "This is a date, not a job interview."

"I know, I know." Joe sighed. "It's been so long, that's all. I don't know what to say or what to do."

"Be yourself, that's all. It'll come naturally to you."

"I don't know why he's interested in me. Callum is so good-looking. He could get a date with anyone."

"Then he must have good taste, because he asked you."

Joe's shyness and lack of confidence became increasingly obvious the more time Elijah spent with him. After lunch yesterday, Elijah excused himself for a few minutes, giving Callum the chance to make a move. Returning from the bathroom, he found Joe fumbling with his phone in an effort to swap numbers with the waiter. Sure, Callum was a handsome young man. Joe was too, but he seemed to have no awareness of it.

He'd relaxed a little when they got to the house. They spent a quiet evening catching up on each other's news. Without the pressure of other people around, he came out of himself, revealing the true degree of his anxiety. He was currently taking antidepressant medication and had been seeing a counselor. For a young man, he had the weight of the world on his shoulders.

All because he'd been in the wrong place at the wrong time.

Elijah hoped his date tonight would go some way to restoring his confidence.

"Just take it easy," Elijah told him. "If it doesn't go to plan, or you don't like each other, what have you lost other than a couple of hours of your time? On the other hand, you might really like him. He seems like a nice guy. Intelligent. Hardworking. Attentive. You have nothing to lose."

Finally, Joe smiled. "You're right. I know. Jesus, this time last year, I used to rock up to meet guys without knowing their name. Sometimes two or three in a week. Now, I'm nervous about a single date."

"You'll be fine," he said, pulling up outside Queens Court in the heart of the gay scene. Elijah opened his wallet and pulled out three ten-pound notes. "Here. That'll get you a taxi back to our place if the night doesn't go to plan. And if it does, well, it'll get you and Callum a couple of rounds of drinks."

"There's no need," Joe protested.

"Take it. My treat. Now go on, have fun."

With an uncertain smile, Joe took the money and got out of the car. Elijah watched him as he walked through the arch into the pub courtyard. He would be all right. A new man and a change of scene would do him good.

A navy BMW sat idling behind Elijah. The windows were tinted and he couldn't make out the driver. *How long has it been there?* he wondered. There was plenty of room for the car to pass him. Immediately the suspicion he had been followed raised itself. Could it be? He hadn't paid attention as he drove here, too concerned about Joe. There was no obvious sign of a camera on the driver, but that didn't mean it wasn't a journalist. He hadn't thought to check as he left the house whether any were lurking around.

And if not a journalist, who? Another fan? A stalker? A heavy for hire?

No, he refused to think like that.

He waited and a moment later, a young woman came out of Queens Court. Laughing, she headed straight for the passenger side of the BMW and climbed in. The driver indicated and pulled out, passing Elijah's car without a glance.

A complete false alarm. He had to quit overreacting. He'd drive himself nuts.

Pulling out, he drove around the corner to the railway station. Daniel's train wasn't due for another ten minutes. Elijah parked and got out of the car. It was another beautiful evening, and the streets were busy with revelers heading into town for Friday night. Nobody bothered him as he waited outside. Elijah was recognized far less often than Daniel, particularly when he didn't want to attract attention.

The cynic in him believed that was because of his ethnicity and the color of his skin. Even in a multicultural city like Leeds, people were less inclined to look twice at a dark-skinned fellow than a perfect white man. Even though he hadn't acted in years, his agent still fielded calls from casting directors looking to fill terrorist roles. Only this year, an A-list director had wanted to see him for a large part in a blockbuster franchise film.

"What's the part?" Elijah asked.

"A Muslim doctor," his agent answered.

"Don't tell me, he's secretly a member of ISIS."

"Afraid so, but they're offering good money for a few days' work."

"I'll hold out for James Bond," he said, putting down the phone. A gay, half-Greek Bond, now that would be worth waiting for.

Just like his comedy career, he'd let go of any aspiration he had to be an actor. His interests and priorities had changed. Performing was a thing of the past.

Daniel arrived a few minutes later, his train on time. He came down the front steps, head bowed in his Poldark disguise.

"Does that actually fool anyone?" Elijah asked, hugging him tight and ruffling the hairpiece.

"I got past two dozen journalists this very morning," he said, copping a feel of Elijah's arse. "And no one bothered me on the train, so I must be doing something right."

"Let's get you home," Elijah said, "because I'd like to be doing you right."

Elijah was pleased when Daniel didn't complain about going back to the house. He'd been so set against the idea when he left for London, he wasn't sure how he would react this evening, but he got into the car without complaining, or even raising the issue.

When Elijah pulled into traffic, Daniel tore off the wig and raked his fingers through his short brown hair. Elijah risked a quick sideways glance at him. His man looked tired.

"Good trip?" he asked.

"Yes and no, I guess. I'm glad I went but I think it's created as many new questions as it answered. Keeley has gone off like a bloodhound again in search of the truth."

"Do you want to talk about it?"

Daniel sighed. "Later. I've been over it in my head a million times on the train, I want to think about something else for a while. Tell me about Joe and this date. He's a fast worker."

"Not really," Elijah said. "Callum was the one to ask him out, and it took a lot of effort to persuade him to go. He was still trying to come up with excuses to call it off an hour ago."

"How come? Is there something wrong with this guy Callum?"

"Not a bit. He seems really nice. I just want Joe to realize that. The poor guy is in a bad place. I'm worried about him.

"What do you mean?"

Elijah guided the car onto the city ring road, turning toward home. "Quiet and withdrawn. His eyes are completely flat, and he's lost all his youthful spark. And he's skinny. Painfully skinny. You should prepare yourself before you see him. I don't know much about eating disorders, but his appearance rings alarm bells."

"Oh, no." Daniel sounded deflated. "Maybe I should speak to his mother. See whether she's picked up on anything."

"Let's see how the weekend goes. He might think we're interfering and that could make him worse, or even secretive. We have to support him, that's all."

"Maybe he isn't ready for this date. Maybe it's too soon."

"Only he can be the judge of that. I trust him to make the right decision."

* * * *

From the doorway of the pub, Joe took one look at the huge crowd of people packed into the narrow bar and considered running straight back to the safety of Elijah's car. Guys stood shoulder to shoulder, while the music blasted, and the sound of raised voices was almost deafening. Panic rose from his stomach and tightened in his chest.

He couldn't do this. There were too many people and too much noise. And despite the crowd, he noticed how several heads turned in his direction to check out the newcomer. The fresh meat.

He stepped back into the courtyard and breathed the fresh air. Very slowly, in and out. Then he closed his eyes and counted to ten, remembering all the techniques he'd learned for dealing with stress.

He could do this. He had to do this.

"Hey, you're not thinking of leaving without me, are you?" said a familiar Geordie voice behind him.

Joe turned to see Callum heading in his direction with a broad grin plastered to his face. He wore jeans and a navy shirt. *Wow*. He was much better-looking than Joe remembered.

Callum's smile faltered as he caught the expression on Joe's face. "Is everything okay?" he asked.

"Fine." Joe swallowed and tried to compose himself. "It's...it's very hot in there, and busy. I'm not too good in crowds." It sounded lame, even to his own ears.

Callum looked over his shoulder into the bar. "I see what you mean," he said, his voice kind. "But everywhere will be packed tonight. Why don't you wait here? I'll get us a couple of drinks and bring them out. What will you have?"

"Vodka and diet tonic."

"Wait here and I'll be right back."

Joe breathed more easily. He couldn't relax but at least he didn't have to walk into that crowd just yet. Maybe later, after a drink or two, he'd feel better about it. He moved into a quiet corner of the courtyard, away from the people who had come outside to smoke, and lit a cigarette of his own. The packet was almost full. He hoped it would be enough to last the night. He always smoked more when he was nervous. Dragging hard, he took the smoke deep into his lungs, held it, then exhaled slowly.

Before the attack, he'd only ever been a social smoker. One or two cheeky fags on a night out and nothing more. Since then, he'd developed a forty-a-day habit—sixty on really bad days. Cigarettes made everything a little easier, giving an incentive to go from one hour to the next. He knew they were no good for his health, waking each morning with a terrible taste in his mouth and an irritating tickle at the back of his throat, but mentally, they were essential. His mother had forbidden him from smoking in the house, so going out to the garden for the first smoke of the day was his reason to get out of bed each morning.

Given a chance, he would take tobacco over food. It did him more good.

Callum returned with the drinks, vodka for Joe and a pint of lager for himself. His face was flushed. "You were right about the crowd in there. It's absolutely packed."

"Thanks." Joe took the drink and offered his pack of smokes.

Callum shook his head. "I don't. But don't let me put you off."

You won't. He watched Callum take a good draught of lager and lick the foam from his upper lip. Callum smiled, showing good white teeth and sparkling eyes. He smelled great too. Sexy and fresh.

"So how long are you in town for?" Callum asked.

"Only a few nights. We're leaving Sunday to go to Durham. That's your neck of the woods, isn't it?"

"Close. I'm from a bit further north. A couple of extra stops on the train, but not too far. Where are you from then?"

"Blackpool."

"God, I love that place. My mam and dad used to take me and my sister for a long weekend every summer."

Joe nodded and waited for Callum to say something else. He realized with horror that he'd lost the knack of making small talk with a stranger. It used to be so easy, the flirting and flattery that came when he met someone for the first time. He fancied Callum — of course he did — but he couldn't think of a way to put it across without sounding awkward. *I've lost my mojo.*

"This is kind of unusual, don't you think?" Callum asked, looking straight into his eyes.

"What do you mean?" Joe broke the gaze and stared at his glass.

"*This*. Going on a date. Most often when I meet someone, I'll already have chatted online, read their profile, looked at their photos, found out what they like and don't, usually seen a few pictures of their dick. But with you, there was nothing. It's a genuine blind date."

"Oh. I see. Is that a problem?"

"Not for me. It's nice actually, but it's unusual for sure. I tried to find you on all the standard social sites but got nothing. You're not an easy boy to get to know."

Joe's face grew hot, and he took a grateful swig of vodka. "I don't have any of those profiles."

"I noticed."

Joe did have a Facebook account. Under an alias, it was a private profile, open to a small group of family members and close friends. He'd shut down all his other social media profiles following the attack in Blackpool. Once he had been named as the boy involved in the Daniel Blake/Elijah Mann story, interest in him had exploded. He had still been in hospital when the photos he'd uploaded of himself in Daniel's room had gone viral. God, the shame of it now. In a jockstrap and cap, spreading his butt cheeks for the world to see.

There was no way to contain it. Although he'd shut down his own accounts, the damn pictures were still out there. He received hundreds of offers from porno producers who wanted to sign him up. The boy at the heart of the story—they all wanted a piece of him. He had an open offer from several studios to become an exclusive model. Before his attack he would have leapt at such an opportunity. He flaunted all he had for free on Twitter and XTube, the idea of becoming a bona fide porn star a dream.

No longer.

It wasn't all porn. He'd been courted by the producers of every cheap, trash, Z-list reality, celebrity TV show going, most of which he'd never heard of. *Celebrity Dating, Celebrity Bodies, Celebrities on an Island, Loved-Up Celebrities – all of it, crap.*

He'd had a taste of major attention and hated it.

"Look," Joe said, taking a deep breath, "let's get this over with. If you searched for my social media profile, it won't have taken you long to find the rest of it. The boy toy who blew a man's brains out."

Callum dropped the smile. "Sorry. I really didn't know who you were when I asked you out. Honestly. I didn't even recognize Elijah when you came in the restaurant. It was only later that the penny dropped."

"Well, now you know. It's all out there. Every gory detail. I need not go over it again. And if it's dick pics you want, there are plenty of those around too, just turn off your adult filters."

Callum put a hand on Joe's forearm. "I am sorry. I shouldn't have brought it up. It was tactless. Stupid."

"It's okay," Joe said, lighting another cigarette. He took a big hit and exhaled. "It's better to get it out in the open straight up. You know how difficult it is to walk down the street, or go into a bar, and see people point at you and whisper? Knowing they're talking about you. That they've read the stories and seen the photos. That they've seen your butt and everything else you've got."

"You shouldn't worry about that. No one cares about pictures."

"I do."

Callum moved closer and lowered his voice. "You shouldn't. Really. If you walked into that bar now, I guarantee you most of the people in there will have cock and arse photos online. Everyone's at it. Instagram is overrun with attention-seeking selfies and wannabe models thirsty for likes. One of the guys I know at college is a porn star, semi-professional anyway. He's done loads of films in London and Manchester. No one cares."

"But has he blown a man's head off?"

Callum moved his hand to Joe's shoulder. It was a brotherly, reassuring gesture. "Blown a man's head off, or saved the lives of three friends? Joe, I'm studying for a degree in law and I know which version I go for. You did the world a favor as far as I see it. I was surprised when I realized who you were, but it changes nothing. I fancied you before I knew any of it and I'm glad you decided to come tonight."

A great, oppressive weight lifted as Joe realized he was glad he'd come too. He looked at Callum with fresh eyes. Not just a beautiful face anymore—there was soul behind those eyes, and understanding. Joe wasn't about to let down his guard completely, but perhaps it was time to lower it a little.

"It's good we got that out the way."

"Listen," Callum said. "I totally get that you're uncomfortable in a crowd like this. We don't have to stay. We can go for a walk, or something to eat. Or there are plenty of nice hotels around, their bars will be quieter than this. Whatever makes you comfortable."

Joe looked around the courtyard. There were about thirty people here now, and as he listened to the pounding music and laughter from inside, a strong sense of determination came over him. He had missed this life. It used to be his world.

He moved close to Callum and put a hand around his waist. "Let's stay a while."

* * * *

Daniel sank his shoulders beneath the hot water of the tub and closed his eyes, breathing in the vapors of his favorite bath salts, allowing his whole mind and body to be still. Completely at peace.

The bath had been Elijah's idea and a good one. "It'll help you to relax," he'd said.

Returning to the house wasn't as bad as Daniel had expected. A few days away had given him some perspective and the upgrade to the security system was impressive. He still had doubts about their long-term future here, but until they made a definite decision, he would stick it out.

Though he'd been looking forward to seeing Joe and was disappointed that he wasn't here, it had been a peaceful evening. He hadn't parted on the greatest terms with Elijah the other morning, but there was no animosity between them now. They were too mature and thought too much of each other to hold a grudge over something so minor. They had conquered bigger problems than a lover's tiff.

A quiet night together was just what they needed. Elijah cooked a lemon chicken risotto while Daniel filled him in on his London trip. They ate the meal with a delicious bottle of Pinot Grigio before Elijah suggested the hot bath to relax him before bed.

Daniel let his concerns drift away in the lavender-scented water. It had been a strange couple of days, but he could say that about most days now. The week ahead would be no different, with the trip to Durham and the gala concert. He had given little thought to the songs he would perform. None of the new material. It would have to be a half-hour set, comprising all the stuff he was well-known for. He'd throw in something from *Lady Lynda* and a handful of covers.

He was looking forward to the event. Max and Ben would be there, and Terry St. King. He hadn't seen Terry in months. It would be good to catch up.

As the water cooled, he got out of the tub, drying himself on an enormous, soft towel. For the first time, he was glad to be home. He couldn't find this kind of comfort in a hotel, no matter how grand or luxurious it was. Some things could only be found at home.

Wrapping the towel around his waist, he headed to the bedroom, stopping short as he reached the door.

Candles of all sizes, from thick cathedral pillars to small tealights, were lit around the room, casting soft, dancing shadows across the walls and bed. The covers were strewn with rose petals.

Elijah, wearing a pair of black briefs with white piping, came toward him with a short glass of whiskey. His taut chest and lean flanks looked beautiful in the candlelight. He handed Daniel the glass and came in for a kiss. He nuzzled his mouth into the nape of Daniel's neck.

"What's all this?" Daniel asked.

"It's for you. To welcome you home. To say I love you."

He raised Elijah's chin to kiss him on the lips. He tasted the potent liquor on his mouth. "I don't need rose petals to know you love me."

"Some things are worth making an effort for." Elijah undid the knot in Daniel's towel. As it fell to the floor, Elijah moved his hand to Daniel's cock, taking the semi-hard length in his palm. "Like this?" He squeezed gently, bringing Daniel to full hardness. "I'm ready," he murmured.

Ready. Daniel pulled back, looking at him seriously. Elijah's dark eyes, always so soulful, glistened with desire and intent. "Are you sure?"

Elijah took Daniel's free hand and guided it to his arse. "Totally ready. I've waited far too long." He tightened his grip on Daniel's dick.

Daniel squeezed Elijah's buttocks. *Oh, man. He has an arse like no one else.* Daniel wanted it more than he ever had, but not if it would hurt Elijah. "I'll go easy on you."

Elijah tugged him with more insistence. "To begin with. Then we'll see how it goes. I want you badly."

"What caused the change of heart?"

"No idea. Something just came over me and I'm bloody glad it did."

Daniel guided him to the bed, heart beating in anticipation. He turned Elijah to face the other way and pressed his body against his back. His cock found its way to the cleft of his butt. Daniel put his hands on Elijah's hips and pressed his mouth to the nape of his neck. Elijah moaned and tipped his head. He shuddered, and gooseflesh prickled beneath Daniel's lips. Daniel teased him, dragging his tongue toward Elijah's ear, feeling his body react and shiver.

Elijah ground his arse against Daniel's dick. There was no doubting how much he wanted it. Daniel tucked his thumbs into the waistband of his underpants and shoved them to mid-thigh. He wrapped a hand around Elijah's pelvis, palm flat on his lower abdomen, and pulled his arse tight against his cock.

Elijah moaned.

"Feel that?" Daniel said, twitching his cock, now sandwiched between Elijah's cheeks. "Is that what you're after?"

Elijah pushed back harder. "Yes," he hissed. "Yes." He broke free of Daniel and leapt onto the bed, rolling onto his back, legs open, an invitation, his cock sticking up against his belly. "Do it now."

Daniel took a bottle of lube from the drawer and climbed between Elijah's thighs. He poured the smooth liquid over his fingers and massaged the opening, going all around the rim, before sliding the tip of a finger inside. Watching Elijah's face for any sign of pain, he went deeper. Elijah bit his bottom lip.

"Okay. Want me to stop?"

Elijah shook his head. "Don't you dare."

Pushing, twisting, withdrawing and going back, Daniel went farther and farther, until his fingers found the smooth nut inside. Elijah let out a long, low groan, and his cock twitched, oozing clear, sticky fluid as Daniel ran his finger over and around his prostate. Elijah wrapped his hands around the back of his knees and drew his legs into his chest, opening wider. He was ready for more.

Daniel squirted more lube into his palm and covered the full length of his cock before positioning himself on top of his man. He lay over him and moved his cock to Elijah's hot, well-prepared opening. Flickering light played across Elijah's face. Daniel saw the furrow of his brow as he entered, but it was pleasure, not pain, etched on his face. Daniel pushed farther and farther until his balls pressed against Elijah's upturned butt, and he was in there all the way.

They were together again. Complete. The barrier, erected between them in the last year, had been broken. Destroyed.

Unlike their love.

Unlike their passion.

They lay together, united, kissing, Daniel stroked Elijah's face, his neck and shoulders rediscovering him, reclaiming him, until their need became too great. Then Daniel gave Elijah what he wanted, fucking him hard and deep. The heat grew fierce. Sweat coated their bodies in a slick film. They shone in the light of the naked flames and reached a shuddering, spurting climax together.

Daniel gripped Elijah as wrenching spasms rode through him.

Satiated. United.

Nothing would come between them again. Daniel would die before he'd let that happen.

Chapter Ten

The A1, traveling north from Leeds to Durham, is one of the most mundane stretches of motorway in the whole of the UK, but Elijah couldn't stop smiling as Daniel negotiated the surprisingly heavy Sunday afternoon traffic. Despite passing through long sections of roadworks and built-up embankments that restricted their view of the scenery, Elijah couldn't have been happier.

He was whole again. In charge of his own mind and body. The damage caused last year had healed. He was over it and in love with Daniel as much as he'd ever been, while Sonny Rock, the man responsible for his injuries, rotted in a graveyard. *We beat you, you bastard. We beat you.*

Joe sat in the back seat of the car. Even he had changed in these last couple of days. There was a twinkle in his olive-green eyes that hadn't been there when he arrived on Thursday. Joe hadn't returned from his date with Callum until midmorning Saturday. He'd sent them a text during the night, letting them know he was fine, that they didn't have to worry. When Joe came through the door with a secretive smile and healthy color in his cheeks, Elijah knew straight away he wasn't the only one who'd been laid that night.

He was pleased for Joe. Whatever happened with Callum would be good for him. His first step back toward a happy, healthy life. His confidence had improved after just a few hours.

And so had Elijah's. Not that it had ever been lacking. He'd always projected a veneer of self-assurance, even when he didn't feel it one hundred percent. But on Friday night, something snapped back into place. Giving himself to Daniel only cemented the healing.

They were survivors. Daniel, Joe and him. Back on top. Back in control. Nothing could beat that feeling.

The sex might even be better than ever. He couldn't keep his hands off Daniel. Since Friday, he wanted him all the time, like a virgin getting it for the first time. His hunger for more was insatiable. Elijah couldn't get enough. Twice more that night, he stroked and sucked Daniel to a perfect state of hardness, before climbing on top and riding him again. He was unstoppable.

The rest of the weekend was no different. Every moment they were alone, Elijah wanted him. In the bathroom, the utility room, on the living room floor. Joe went out late on Saturday to meet Callum after his shift at the restaurant. With the house to themselves, Elijah told Daniel to take him on the staircase.

"Aren't you sore?" Daniel asked, easing Elijah's trousers down and kissing his butt.

"Not yet," Elijah had replied, widening his knees and assuming the position. They had a lot of time to make up.

Elijah wanted him again. Right now. On this boring motorway. If Joe wasn't sitting back there, he'd urge Daniel to pull over and take him. He shifted in his seat and, with one discreet motion, adjusted his throbbing hard-on.

The gesture didn't go unnoticed. He caught the slight turn of Daniel's head, followed by a cheeky smile.

"Got a problem?" Daniel asked.

"Just getting comfortable," he replied coolly. "Try keeping your eyes on the road."

Daniel chuckled. "Seeing as it's so scenic and all."

"How much further?" asked Joe from the back seat.

"Not far," Daniel said.

The journey from Leeds to Durham seldom took more than ninety minutes, even in heavy traffic, but today had taken much longer. They were approaching the exit for Darlington.

"I've played some nice gigs in Darlington," Elijah remarked, trying to take his mind off sex.

"Me too," Daniel said. "It's a beautiful theatre. I've always had a great response from audiences there."

"We should call in on the way back. It'll be nice to look around the town. I haven't been there in quite a few years."

Joe groaned. "Can we get where we're going first, before thinking about the boring drive back?"

The satnav guided Daniel off the A1 and across various winding country roads until they reached the A19. After a couple more junctions, he was off again and onto more rural lanes.

"This place must be in the middle of nowhere," Elijah said, opening the envelope of information they'd been given.

"At least the scenery's improved," Daniel observed as they went through a small village at the foot of a green, sloping hill. In the distance, they could see a blue horizon of sea and sky.

Elijah glanced at the glossy brochure. Rockcliffe Manor, their destination, looked fancy enough. Built in 1802, the literature stated, the grand house stood in four hundred and fifty acres of private grounds right on the Durham coast. It boasted an eighteen-hole golf course, three function rooms, two bars, two restaurants, a walled rose garden, plus the usual spa, gym and beauty facilities found in all good country hotels. Besides the main building, there was also a separate lodge, pub and holiday cottage within the grounds.

"Who found this place?" Daniel asked, turning onto a narrower, tree-lined road. "It's so far from the beaten path. Wouldn't somewhere in the city serve the purpose better?"

"I wanted to get away from the city," Elijah said, stuffing the paperwork back into the envelope. "I thought you would too. Being nearer the sea. I heard there are some fantastic coastal walks around here. April suggested the venue. She sent a list of options and available dates, and this one stood out. Don't you like it?"

"Sure, I do. It seems like a tough sell, that's all. Getting people to come all the way out here."

"It can't have been that tough. The tickets sold out fast enough. The hotel is full too. People must be up for a weekend in the country. Great food, top-drawer entertainment, doing your part for charity. April claims she could have sold the event ten times over. The waiting list for cancelations is huge."

"They should have charged more for the tickets," Joe said.

"They're charging enough," Elijah told him. "I didn't want this to become an elite thing that only the mega-rich could afford."

"What about the press?" Daniel asked. "It won't be crawling with photographers, will it?"

"Relax, we're covered. One official photographer to cover the event. They're from a local lifestyle magazine. No other press allowed. They won't get any farther than the main gate, April assured me of that."

"I hope April is as efficient as she sounds," Daniel said.

"Efficient? After my dealings with her on the phone, I hope she's not as scary as she sounds."

* * * *

April Evie waited for them at the entrance of the manor house. Though he hadn't seen her before, Elijah knew exactly who she was, as she crunched purposefully across the graveled drive before they had gotten out of the car. *How long has she been waiting?* he wondered.

"Elijah. Daniel. So good to meet you at last," she said, bright smile showing perfectly even, brilliant white teeth. Her cheerful voice failed to make up for the blank, Botoxed mask of her face. Her handshake was firm, unbreakable.

Whatever expectations he'd had about April, this was not it.

He guessed her age around forty-five, but it was impossible to be sure, she'd had so much work done. The tight eyes, enlarged lips, petite nose—nothing about her face looked natural. Her hair fell past her shoulders in soft, coppery curls. She wore a light, sleeveless top revealing toned, tan arms, immaculate black slacks and fuck-me shoes that looked very impractical on the loose gravel. He saw a narrow gold watch on one wrist and a multitude of gold bangles on the other.

Elijah realized he was staring and forced his attention back to her face, which was no less startling on second impression. *Has she modeled her entire look on Melania Trump?*

"Good to put a face to a name after all this time," he said.

April opened her mouth and laughed. Apart from a narrowing of her eyes, no other part of her face moved. "That's where I have an advantage over you. I knew exactly what you looked like, only you're both more handsome in the flesh."

Elijah decided that she must have had a fresh dose of Botox this week in time for the gala, because her features were as fixed as a doll's. He caught the bemused look in Daniel's eyes as he came around the car to greet her with an embrace and a double-air kiss.

"So good to meet you," he said. "Seems like it's been a long time coming."

"Gosh, yes," April said. "After all this planning, I can't believe by Wednesday morning it will all be over. So much time and effort focused on a single night. But it'll be worth it. I have no doubt about that. I think this will be the best event I've ever organized."

"We'll make certain it is," Elijah assured her.

"Let me show you around," she said.

Daniel made a move to take their cases out of the car.

"Leave them," April told him. "Someone will take them up to your suite. The honeymoon suite. It's quite beautiful. You've got the best view of the entire manor."

"Hey," Joe said, holding his mobile phone aloft. "The signal out here sucks. And there's no 4G coverage. I told Callum I'd call him when we got here."

"There's Wi-Fi inside," April told him. "But if you want to make a call, you'll get better reception on the other side of the house, around the rose garden." She gestured to the right.

"Okay." Joe nodded, already hastening in that direction. "I'll catch you guys later."

"Young love," Daniel explained as April led them to the main entrance. "Very young love."

"I can almost remember what that's like," April deadpanned. "It was long ago."

From the outside, Rockcliffe Manor was a picture-perfect nineteenth-century country house, set in wide grounds with woodland on one side, a golf course on the other and the North Sea behind it. Elijah's heart sank a little as they entered the main reception room. Not a trace of the original interior remained. The tiled floor, granite-topped reception desk, leather furnishings and modern lighting were like any other contemporary hotel. The walls were adorned with bland black-and-white photos of international city skylines. No part of the hall reflected any of its two-hundred-year history, or its rural Durham location. It could have been anywhere. *What a shame.*

"Wonderful, isn't it?" April gushed. "The present owners took over the place in 2016 and spent millions on the refurbishments, dragging the tired old building into the modern age. You should have seen the state of the place before. There were dowdy wooden panels on all the walls and these horrible old paintings. I would never have suggested it as a party venue back them, but now it's got a real wow factor. Don't you think?"

"I'd like to have seen it before," he said.

April's mouth fell open in a gesture he took for surprise. "No, darling, you wouldn't. Take it from me. It was simply awful. I came to a wedding here once, and it was so grim. The marriage lasted less than a year and I'm not surprised, starting their life together here. That was then, of course. I'm sure if they got married here today, they'd have a long and happy marriage."

Elijah stifled a laugh. April, he'd decided, was fabulous. Utterly ridiculous, but fabulous.

"Have you hosted many events here?" Daniel asked.

"Yes, don't worry. They'll look after us. If they know what's good for them. Unfortunately, this evening and tomorrow, the hotel is open to the public. We'll just have to put up with people using the golf course, ladies coming in for spa days and afternoon tea, but on Tuesday, ahead of the gala, we have exclusive use of the entire hotel. No one gets in without a ticket. Come on, let me show you around."

The rest of the facilities were as bland and corporate as the foyer suggested. Elijah wondered why the place was so popular. It was nice enough for what it was. The refurbishments had been done to a high specification, but other than the grounds and the exterior views, they offered nothing that couldn't be found in any five-star hotel chain.

He chided himself for being so snobby. They were here now and should make the most of it. He wouldn't have to do any real work until Tuesday. Tonight and tomorrow, they could just enjoy themselves.

The main hall where the gala would take place was suitably large, with tall windows and French doors at either end of the room. It was bare at that moment, apart from the stage.

"This will all be dressed tomorrow," April explained. "Round tables, sound equipment, everything will be in place by the evening."

"What about the band?" Daniel asked. "When can I do a rehearsal?"

"The musical director will be here tomorrow afternoon to discuss set lists and anything else you might require. But the full band won't be here until Tuesday morning. I hope that's all right."

"Fine," Daniel answered. "It's no less preparation than I used to get on the cruise ships. I know what I want to sing, it's just a matter of bringing the band up to speed."

"Excellent." April's mouth stretched into an uncomfortable-looking smile.

Elijah perked up when she showed him the kitchen. The facilities were more than he'd expected. It made Kostas' kitchen in Corfu look like a closet. A full refit of the cooking area had been part of the hotel's vast refurbishment. It was one area of modernization he wouldn't complain about. There was plenty of surface space and he spotted at least four catering-sized ovens.

"Fantastic." He beamed, looking around. "It's amazing."

"There's also this." April led him toward a large, stainless-steel door. "Open it."

He gripped the huge metal handle and tugged, pulling the door outward, to reveal the biggest larder he'd ever seen. Stocked to bursting, it was a cook's dream. There was an entire market stall's worth of fresh vegetables and fruit, while the shelves above were stocked with tins, jars and bottles.

"This is amazing," he gasped. "I feel like I'm on *Celebrity Top Cook* again."

"The meat and fresh seafood are due to be delivered in the morning. The hotel's head chef, Magda, will also meet you to talk through your menu and show you where everything is. Magda is a phenomenal woman, but on the night she'll act as your sous chef. You'll oversee the kitchen and run the operation."

"Shit." Elijah was suddenly struck by the enormity of the task. *What the hell have I let myself in for?* The kitchen, his menu, a room full of VIPs all expecting the best of him. This had seemed so much easier when it was an idea in his head, or a few scribbled notes. And who was this Magda? Chefs were a formidable breed. Having reached the top job in the restaurant, he couldn't imagine her taking instructions from him, a talented amateur.

This was a much bigger deal than he'd expected.

But wasn't that what he wanted? A challenge. A chance to reinvent himself. Throw off an old life and embrace a new one.

He'd been given a chance like no other. He'd better not fuck it up.

* * * *

The North Sea crashed against the rocky outcrop of a wide cove, throwing white spume into the air. They were a long way from the balmy beaches of Corfu they'd recently gotten used to. A strong wind cut through Elijah's clothes and he was grateful he'd taken heed of Daniel and grabbed his navy bomber jacket before leaving the hotel. It was early evening and the blue sky had already darkened in color toward dusk.

It was Elijah's idea to get out of the hotel for an hour before dark set in, and they'd be confined to the grounds. They had followed the path from the rear of the house and after five minutes their effort was rewarded as they reached the edge of the cliff and the wide, rolling expanse of the sea.

"This is great," Daniel said, taking Elijah's hand as they faced into the wind.

Elijah took a deep breath, filling his lungs with the fresh, salty air. "Yeah, this does make it worthwhile," he said, "because the hotel sucks."

"It's not that bad," Daniel said, nudging his shoulder. "It's everything we need to host a charity gig."

"They've ripped the soul out of the place. It's so disappointing. Depressing, in fact. I wanted a grand country house. This could be anywhere."

"April seems pretty enamored by it."

"Is it any wonder? She's hardly an advocate for natural beauty, is she?"

"Now, now. Don't be bitchy. She's kind of sweet."

"Until Trump realizes we've stolen the Melania-bott."

"I wonder what she looked like before? People who've had so much work never look prettier or younger, just kind of weird. I bet she didn't need it in the first place."

"I know nothing about her, except she's bloody good at her job. Personally, I think she bummed out with the venue, but that's just my taste. I doubt any of the guests will complain."

"They'll have nothing to complain about. Great dinner and a great show, we'll deliver on both counts."

The line of the cliff sloped down to the shore. They left the footpath to walk along the sand.

It struck Elijah for the first time that they hadn't seen another person since leaving the house. That made this place even more perfect. As April had finished the tour of the facilities, he'd spotted a group of ladies in the tea room leap to attention as they realized who they were. They had hurried through before the women reached for their phones. He wanted time alone with Daniel before they had to spring into full celebrity mode on Tuesday.

"Feel like a little beach-front action?" he asked, squeezing Daniel's hand.

Daniel's eyebrows shot up in surprise. "Here? Are you mad? We'll freeze our balls off. You know that's not the Mediterranean out there?"

"I know a good way to keep your balls warm." He winked.

"Save it for the hotel. I am not dropping my pants out here."

"Spoilsport."

"You're insatiable."

"Just making up for lost time."

"I noticed. You can make it up later. In the shower, in bed, anywhere warm will do."

"That had better be a promise."

Farther along the coast, set back from the beach, they found a small holiday cottage. Standing alone, it had the most perfect view of the sea.

"Wow," Daniel said, approaching the front path. "This is beautiful. Do you think it's part of the hotel?"

"I dunno." Elijah moved closer to peer through the curtained window. He couldn't see much inside apart from a small living room, dominated by a single sofa and a fireplace. "It's got to be a holiday let of some kind. It doesn't look lived in enough to be someone's home."

"I wonder if it's available."

Elijah liked the authentic appearance of the interior, even though it was small. If the cottage was part of Rockcliffe Manor, the modernization hadn't extended this far. It had the old-world charm the main house was lacking. "Did I ever tell you that I've always wanted to get screwed in a fisherman's cottage?"

"I don't remember you ever saying so."

"It's a lifelong ambition."

"The mood you're in, you'd want to get screwed anywhere."

"True," he said, slipping his hand around Daniel's waist. "This place seems unoccupied. If it's part of the hotel, I don't see why we can't move in. Let's find out if it's available."

With an arm around each other, they headed back along the cove.

Just the two of them alone on a beach. For Elijah, it didn't get much better than that.

Chapter Eleven

The following morning was a mild one with a light wind coming from the north-west. After breakfast, Daniel spent most of his time alone in the rose garden with his notebook. Its protective walls shielded him from the breeze and he could almost imagine he was back in Corfu.

It was disappointing to learn the cottage on the beach they had discovered last night fell beyond the grounds of the hotel.

"I can find out who owns it," April told them when they inquired about its availability. "If it's empty, we may be able to get you in there."

He told her not to bother. They were staying only two nights, it wasn't worth the effort. Besides, their friends were arriving today, and they were staying in the main house. It would be better if they were all together.

Elijah had gone off to meet the hotel chef and discuss arrangements for tomorrow, while Joe had told him the night before he intended to stay up late, chatting with Callum, and would like to lie in this morning. In a matter of days he seemed to have fallen head over heels for the waiter. Daniel worried that Joe might be rushing into things too fast—he was vulnerable, and he didn't want to see him get hurt—but then he remembered just how fast he had fallen in love with Elijah. It was impossible to put a timescale on such powerful emotions. Love developed when it was ready. It couldn't be forced or denied.

Daniel spent the morning in the garden working on the lyrics to a new song. The setting inspired him. He knew nothing about growing plants or different types of flowers, but could still appreciate the beauty here. The variety of color in the roses surprised him, from traditional reds, pinks and white, to orange petals, purple, and black and one rose was a most magnificent shade of royal blue. Every half-hour, he would put down his book and rise to stretch his legs and spine, taking a couple of leisurely walks around the outer path each time. He didn't see another person the whole time he was there.

Around one o'clock, he'd had enough and made his way back to the house in search of coffee.

April was waiting for him in the foyer. Daniel did a double-take when he saw her. In a tight gray skirt and sheer black blouse with a leopard-print scarf and matching high heels, she looked glamorously formidable.

"Daniel, darling, where have you been? I've looked everywhere for you."

"Outside, in the garden."

She regarded him with a frozen expression. No doubt wondering why he would go outside for anything other than a game of golf or a cigarette when her ritzy hotel had so much to offer inside.

"To take selfies?" she asked at last.

"No," he said, bemused. "To write." He held up his notebook.

April's face did not change. "Lindy, the musical director, is here. Would you like to meet her? To go over your program of music?"

"Absolutely. I'd just like to grab a coffee first."

"Oh, we'll have that brought through." She turned a sharp head and snapped her fingers at the receptionist. "Coffee," she barked. "Have it brought to the main hall at once."

"I can get my own," he said, horrified.

April linked her arm in his and guided him away. "You're a star. You shouldn't have to do anything for yourself. Certainly nothing as menial as that. Besides, people want to do things for stars like you. So, let them. Believe me, fetching coffee for Daniel Blake will make her little day."

So, he realized, that was the kind of woman April was. Kissing the arse of those she thought were important while stomping over the ones she thought beneath her. "That's not the way I treat people," he said with defiance.

April squeezed his arm, dismissing the matter. He made a mental note to stop by later and apologize to the receptionist. He wouldn't let her think the demanding attitude was his.

"Now," April said, "Lindy Wardale is a big deal. She's a conductor with the North-East Sinfonia. She's had a wonderful career playing all over the world — the USA, Europe, Russia. She's conducted at the Royal Opera House and the English National Opera."

"Wow," he said, impressed. "I didn't expect someone so big."

"This will be a special night." April preened. "And, best of all, Lindy is giving her time and services completely for free. Not only that, but we'll have ten members of her orchestra here tomorrow. No dodgy backing tracks. This will be a fully live experience."

"That's incredible."

"I know," she said without a trace of modesty.

In the main hall, a grand piano had been set on the stage. A tall woman in her late forties stood beside it, sorting through large pages of sheet music. Her head rose as they entered. Keen eyes peered at Daniel over the top of tortoise-shell spectacles. April made the introductions before leaving them alone.

"I had no idea we were getting a classical house band," Daniel said enthusiastically. "I thought a keyboard and a drum set if we were lucky. This is a real honor."

"This charity means a lot to me," Lindy said. "The work they do is essential and under-appreciated. When they asked me to get involved, I jumped at the chance. I didn't even know who was performing when I said yes. Daniel Blake, Max LaFranchi and Terry St. King. That's quite a bill. Believe me, Daniel, this is a big honor for me too."

Lindy had a deep, flat-sounding voice that failed to get across the excitement of her words, but her eyes were kind and her smile, wide and upturned, seemed genuine. Despite her position of authority, she couldn't have been more different from April in her appearance and dress. April's designer wardrobe and towering heels were all about appearance and projecting an image of control. In contrast, Lindy's flat shoes and long flowing skirt were for comfort. She gave off a confident vibe that said she was here to do a job, not look like a million dollars.

"This fundraiser was my partner's idea," Daniel explained. "Elijah deserves all the credit. He wanted to do something for Supporting Victims North East."

"I'm glad he did. The charity is invaluable, but funds are scarce. There's only so much money to go around and people are always more willing to give to hospitals or cancer charities. I used to be the same. Most people don't think about victim support until they need the service themselves."

Lindy had her own story, Daniel guessed. So many people did. He didn't press for details. She would tell as much as she wanted when she was ready. He knew from experience how well-meaning questions were more often an irritant than a comfort.

Tell me what happened? It must be so difficult. Any time you need to talk, you know where I am.

He'd heard it all. If Lindy had suffered trouble of her own, she'd have heard it too.

"So, how is this going to work?" he asked.

"I'm afraid there isn't much time to rehearse," she said, taking a seat at the piano.

"I'm used to it." He told her of his time at sea. "It wasn't unusual to join a ship in the afternoon, have a one-hour run-through with the band, then put on a show for the audience that evening. Terry is used to working that way too. And I don't think Max will need much practice. She can put on a show the moment she gets out of bed."

Lindy drew back her long blonde hair, streaked with gray, and fastened it with a rubber band. "Then this should be a breeze for everyone. So, what about your set list? Do you have your own music with you?"

He nodded, opening his notebook. "I've got sheet music in my room, but this is what I planned to do."

For the next twenty minutes they worked through his song selection. Lindy was familiar with most of them. Their coffee arrived as they played around with the numbers. He found it exciting. Sparking off an MD, planning a show. The prospect of working with Lindy and her orchestra, albeit reduced in size, was a thrill. She promised him a balanced selection of players.

"String section, brass, percussion. In a room like this, it will sound amazing. Your guests are in for a treat."

At that moment a new voice cut across the hall.

"Of course they are, dear girl. It's the crème de la crème of the showbusiness world. It'll be fab-u-lous."

The nasal, New Zealand tones were unmistakable. Terry St. King had arrived. He stood in the doorway, feet poised, arms raised, a vision in a white jacket and pants. Pure theater.

He knew how to make an entrance.

Daniel ran at him with open arms and caught himself from hugging the older man too tight. The body beneath the clothes was tiny. It felt as if he were holding on to nothing but skin and bone. Terry had always been skinny but each time they met he appeared a little frailer than the time before. But there was nothing weak about his attitude.

"It's good to see you," Daniel said, stepping back to inspect the man who had saved his life.

Terry smiled, self-deprecatingly, showing his famous, oversized teeth. He'd taken to wearing a wig, and it appeared too large for his head. His face was small and drawn beneath it. Daniel noticed that his jacket was also too large and hung off his shoulders. A tight sensation gripped Daniel's guts. Terry didn't just look frail — he looked unwell.

There was no point asking about his health. Terry would never admit to his failings. Some things, like his age, were a close-guarded secret. He could see things were not right with the old boy, but getting to the bottom of it would not be easy. He'd have to tread carefully.

"I wouldn't have missed this for anything," Terry made a grand gesture around the room. "It's so exciting. Is everything set?"

"Pretty much," Daniel told him. "I was just running through my set list with Lindy."

"Ah." Terry clapped bejeweled hands together. "You've got a proper piano. That's marvelous. I was worried I might have to play on some two-bit keyboard. Muriel."

At the sound of her name, Terry's long-suffering PA, Muriel Durrell, came into the hall, dragging a large trolley case behind her.

"Did you bring my music, Muriel?" Terry asked archly. "Look, darling, they've got a real piano for me to play on."

"Yes," she said. "I've got your music. Do you want it now?"

"Of course I don't. I'm just making sure that you have it."

"I do." She sighed.

"Good."

Daniel embraced the older woman. Her broad, cuddly figure only highlighted how skinny Terry had become. She held him tight, pressing her bosom against his chest.

"Hello, Daniel."

She stepped back, adjusted her horn-rimmed glasses and patted her short, ash-blonde hair. Though she was younger than Terry, most women her age would have retired by now, but Muriel seemed happy following him around and organizing his life. Daniel often wondered how either of them would cope without the other.

"Did you see Terry on *The One Show* the other week?"

"No, I've been away all summer. I only got back to the UK last week."

"I saw it," Lindy said, stepping down from the stage. "You were on fine form."

Terry and Muriel regarded her with fixed, icy stares.

"And who might you be?" Terry asked in an icy tone.

"Drop the bitchy-queen act," Daniel interjected. "Lindy is the conductor with the North-East Sinfonia. She's our MD."

That bit of information brightened Terry in an instant. "Oh, how marvelous. I'm glad you're here. I want to sing some songs from my new album. Show them, Muriel."

She bent over, unlocked the case and pulled out copies of a book and album. Daniel stifled a laugh as he looked at the camp image that adorned the covers of both. Terry reclined on top of a giant disco ball, kicking his legs in the air. It was ridiculous.

"It's the revised and expanded paperback edition of my autobiography," he announced proudly. "When I knew it was coming out I had the marvelous idea of releasing a tie-in CD. A unique interpretation of my all-time favorite songs. What do you think?"

The book was called *Glitter Balls — From the Gutter to the Glitz — The Extraordinary Life of Terry St. King*. Terry had sent a copy of the hardback when it came out last

Christmas. To his shame, Daniel hadn't read it yet. He knew it contained a long section dedicated to that night on *The Atlantic Anthem*. After the attack on Elijah in Blackpool, he couldn't face going through it again.

The companion-piece album was a collection of cover versions. Songs that "play an important part in the soundtrack of my life," the blurb stated. An eclectic bag. Daniel recognized tunes from various musicals, together with pop and disco tracks.

"*Dance Yourself Dizzy* is the lead single." Terry beamed. "We've got remixes and everything. I believe it's what they call a banger. If Max LaFranchi can do it, I don't see why I can't."

"No." Daniel laughed. "Neither can I."

"I'm hoping they'll let me perform it on this year's *Strictly*. Now, Muriel, get me a pen so I can sign these for Daniel and Lindy."

The tension in Daniel's guts faded as Terry made a grand show of signing the books and CDs. He might look a little older, a little weaker, but there was nothing holding him back. It was good to have him here.

Last night and this morning, Daniel had thought he wanted to be alone. He realized now that was stupid. He wanted—no, needed—his friends around him. Terry and Joe were here. Max and Ben were on their way.

As long as he had friends, people like Oliver and Sonny would never bring him down.

Two nights with them all together. They would have the best time. He'd make sure of it. No one was going to spoil it.

* * * *

144

Daniel went up to the bedroom to collect his mobile phone from the charger before meeting Elijah for lunch. As he checked the display, he discovered he had four missed calls from Keeley.

He called straight back and was connected to her voicemail. He hung up and dialed his own message service. Keeley had left a message half an hour ago.

"Hi. Just calling to let you know there's been a change of plan. I'm on my way to Blackpool. I've got a lead on Sonny Rock. Someone who served time in prison with him in the nineties. Says he's got information but it'll cost. It might be nothing but a con-trick, but I figured it's worth the effort to find out. I'm heading north for your show anyway so it's only a couple of hours out of my way. I'll call you later if there's anything to report."

Keeley was supposed to be on the trail of Rachel's ex-husband. He wondered where this new lead had come from. Whether it would be worth the effort?

He listened to the message again before deleting it. They'd been led on before by people who claimed to have inside knowledge of Sonny, or Oliver, or his birth mother. None of it had ever checked out. There was no reason to believe this new lead would be any different.

But Keeley would leave no stone unturned. He trusted her instincts. If there was anything to be gained, she would find it.

Daniel pocketed his phone and went downstairs to find Elijah.

Chapter Twelve

Josh Jackson, owner of the Cellar Steps restaurant, stood at the front door as the party of famous guests arrived. The Cellar Steps had an awesome reputation for its seasonal food, first-class wine list and excellent service. Elijah first heard about it while competing on *Celebrity Top Cook*, and it had been high on his list of must-try places ever since. When he realized how close Rockcliffe Manor was to the restaurant, he'd phoned ahead to book a table for Monday night.

He'd asked Josh to sit them in a quiet area, away from the main crowd.

If observed, their party would cause a stir and the last thing they needed was someone tipping off the press. Or, worse, recording their conversations and uploading them to the internet. Their group comprised Daniel and himself, Terry, Muriel, Joe and April, together with Max and Ben, who'd arrived late that afternoon.

Josh, a good-looking blond man in his early thirties, greeted him with a firm handshake, before leading the group down a narrow staircase with a low ceiling. The main entrance, found on the cobbles of Sadler Street, was deceiving, as the restaurant was situated below, within the thirteenth-century cellars, and retained the original stone features and archways. On the far side of the room, large windows looked down on the river.

"Wow," Max said behind him. "This place is really something."

"Isn't it just?" Elijah agreed. He'd heard a lot of good things about the Cellar Steps, about its history and the food, but this surpassed his expectations.

This is the kind of place I want, he thought, looking around at the candlelit tables, the tucked-away booths, the exquisite plates of food that were being served. To own a restaurant like this was the big dream. Somewhere like no other. Places like the modernized Rockcliffe Manor, bland identikit eateries, could be found anywhere, in any city, in any country. When Elijah got around to opening his own place, this would be the standard to aim for. Somewhere historic, beautiful and unique.

Sensing his awe, Daniel came closer and took his hand. "Like it?"

"I love it," Elijah said. He counted on the food living up to the setting.

"It's a pleasure to have you all here." Josh showed them to a table in a private alcove. "I'm looking forward to the show and dinner tomorrow night."

"Of course," April said as Josh pulled out her chair. "I thought there was something familiar about your name. Mr. Jackson has bought a table for ten tomorrow evening," she explained for the benefit of the others.

"Supporting Victims is an important charity. We do everything we can to raise funds for the cause."

"We'll be sure to put on a hell of a great show," Max said with real enthusiasm. "Especially for you."

"I'm never less than great," Terry said tartly. "Every show is my best."

Elijah realized Max and Terry were sitting next to each other. He hoped that would work out. He couldn't be bothered with any of their diva behavior or one-upmanship. Not tonight.

"I know it is," Max said, placing a tactful hand on top of Terry's. "I saw you at the Crazy Coq last year and you were fabulous, darling."

"Thank you, my dear." Terry smiled, displaying his gigantic white teeth.

Daniel had warned Elijah about Terry's weight loss, but it didn't prepare him for just how terrible he looked in person. His whole head appeared to have shrunk around his teeth.

With the table seated, two waiters arrived to charge their glasses with champagne.

"A present from the house," the head waiter said as he poured.

"That's the kind of welcome we like," Max said, beaming at the young man who filled her glass.

Yeah, this was a good idea. Elijah had been disheartened when they had arrived at the hotel yesterday. At how bland and soulless the place was. He'd spent most of today in the kitchen with Magda, the head chef, running through the menu and practicalities of service. Tomorrow would involve a huge amount of work. He was anxious and knew he'd wouldn't sleep much tonight. An evening of good company was just what he needed.

So far, the place had outstripped his expectations.

* * * *

Joe checked his phone for the dozenth time. He'd left it alone for the few minutes it took to eat his starter, but as soon as the plates were cleared, it was in his hand again. He was starting to piss Daniel off.

"Can't you leave it?" Daniel asked, failing to hide the irritation he felt. He should have stayed at the hotel if all he wanted to do was text.

"Can't get a proper signal," Joe answered petulantly.

"That's an even better reason to put it down," he said with firmness.

Joe finally got the message and stuck the handset in his pocket.

"I thought you said Callum was working tonight."

"He is."

"Then he'll hardly have time to message you, will he?"

"Leave him alone," Max said, stepping in to keep the peace. "Joe's been bitten by the bug, that's all. Badly I think. When can I meet the lucky guy?"

"Tomorrow," Joe said, perking up. "His train gets in at noon." He turned his attention back to Daniel. "Can I borrow the car? I want to pick him up from the station."

"Of course you can," Elijah answered for him.

"Just a minute," Daniel said. "I might need it myself."

"It'll only take an hour. Ninety minutes tops," Joe said. "We'll come straight back to the hotel."

"You won't need it," Elijah said to Daniel. "You'll be tied up in rehearsals most of the day."

He was right, of course. Daniel would require all the time he could get with the band when they arrived. *Why am I so pissed?* He should be in the best of moods.

His friends were all here and Elijah was treating them to this fantastic meal. *So, what is it?*

Keeley's phone call bothered him more than he'd first thought. Not being able to speak to her, to find out exactly what her lead was about, didn't help his mood. To begin with, he'd dismissed it as nothing to get worked up about, but the more he pondered this development, the harder he found it to ignore. It was possible, more than possible, that the man she was going to meet had been in prison with Sonny, that he knew about the person who'd hired him and could even identify them.

He resisted the temptation to check his phone for another message. Having just bawled out Joe, he could hardly do the same thing. He'd tried it when they first sat down. Joe was right. The signal sucked.

Damn. Now he flushed with guilt. He peered at Joe, at those injured, olive eyes. The boy had had a dreadful time and now he'd found the first inkling of happiness, Daniel was acting like a prissy bitch.

"Sorry," Daniel told him. "Of course you can have the car. For as long as you like. Take Callum to lunch. It'll be my treat."

Daniel sighed and took a long drink of wine.

Under the table, Elijah moved his hand to Daniel's thigh and gave it a tender squeeze. "Everything okay?"

"Fine," Daniel replied, keeping his voice low, so the others couldn't hear. "Just uptight, that's all. I'll get over it."

Elijah squeezed again and leaned closer. His breath was warm on Daniel's cheek.

"I love you," he said.

After that, Daniel felt better.

On the other side of him sat Ben. In a short-sleeved, open-neck shirt, Ben looked as if he were still in the honeymoon/holiday mood. Daniel caught the way his eyes focused on Max farther around the table, watching her adoringly.

"How does it feel to be home?" Daniel asked him.

"I'm still not used to being on dry land after all those weeks at sea. I can still feel the motion of the boat even though everything is still."

"It's in your blood now," Daniel said. "The love for the sea will never leave you. You'll always want to go back."

"I don't doubt that. We're already looking to hire a boat for a Christmas or New Year getaway."

"You're definitely hooked then."

"How's your writing going?"

"Good. I'm still working on new material."

"Cool. I've got a couple of days free next week. Why don't you come to the studio and record a few demos? See how they play out."

"I'd love to." Daniel's diary was open for the next few weeks. Despite the extended summer holiday, he'd refused to allow his manager to inundate him with work afterward. He'd need space to develop his new songs, as well as cooperate with Keeley on the book. The show tomorrow night would be his only live performance for the rest of the year.

"Daniel, darling," Terry called across the table. "I haven't had a chance to ask yet, but I read about the incident with that little trog-let in your bedroom. What on earth happened there?"

Next to Terry, Max also spoke up. "God, yes. How the hell did she get in? I thought you had the house locked up tight."

"It was nothing," he said, playing the event down. Lauren Warwick had ruined his return from holiday. She would not wreck this meal. "An over-enthusiastic fan. Nothing to worry about."

Terry grimaced. "They're getting worse. People think they own us. This would never have happened in the good old days. Stars had a certain level of mystique then. An aloofness. Fans respected it and maintained their distance. Now it's all bloody selfies and Instagram. Can you imagine pestering Shirley Bassey or Liberace for a selfie? They wouldn't do it. But now people expect it. And if you don't give them what they want, they scream abuse at you. One moment it's 'Terry, darling, we love you so much' and the next it's 'You stuck-up, old queen.' No class. That's what's wrong these days. Nobody has got any damn class."

"It's not that bad," Max said, placating him. "Most people are lovely. It's just a tiny minority who spoil things."

Terry screwed up his face. "It's the minority we have to worry about. I don't go near social media. Muriel takes care of all my posts, don't you, dear? But, God, darling, when I do look at all, it's nothing but filth and nastiness. I like a good bitch as much as anyone, but the stuff people write goes way beyond that."

Throughout the meal, Daniel noticed how Terry did a lot of talking and little eating. He took a couple of small sips of soup and when his main course arrived, he pushed the contents around the plate with his fork, but never once took it to his mouth. When he raised his glass of wine, he seemed to have difficulty swallowing. His makeup was powdered on heavily tonight, but it couldn't disguise the skeletal features of the face beneath.

When Muriel excused herself to go to the bathroom, Daniel did the same, catching up with her in the hall.

"Muriel," he called. "Hold on a minute."

Terry's PA turned warily toward him, peering at him through the opaque lenses of her glasses. She wore a brown, roll-neck sweater beneath a snug tweed suit. The buttons on her jacket strained across her enormous breasts.

"What a lovely meal this is," she said, sounding humble and avoiding his eyes. "It was kind of you to invite us."

"Don't be silly. We're all friends. And Terry's been so generous, giving us a show tomorrow."

Muriel backed against the wall and glanced down the corridor, toward the sanctuary of the ladies' bathroom, looking nervous. "Terry lives to perform," she said.

Daniel stepped closer, lowering his voice. "But Terry isn't well, is he? You can tell me, Muriel. I saw it the moment he arrived. He's not his old self. He's trying to act like he is, but that's all it is. An act."

"I'm quite sure I don't —"

"Muriel," he urged. "C'mon on. That man saved my life. If there's something wrong with him, I want to know. I want to help."

Muriel's chest sank. She sighed. "You can't help. Just...just say nothing. He'd be mortified if he knew you knew. Let him maintain the act and do the show tomorrow. That's the best way you can help him."

Daniel's thighs weakened. He tightened his core, needing to appear stronger. "What is it?"

She peered furtively back to the main room. "Cancer," she whispered.

Oh God, no.

"Where?" he asked.

"His pancreas."

Deflated, Daniel put a hand on the stone wall. "What...? How far...?"

"The tumor was advanced by the time they found it. Terry had an operation in the spring, which removed most of it. Now he's undergoing chemo to prevent the growth or spread of what remains."

It all made sense. The wig, the makeup. Terry didn't wear them because of vanity. They were hiding the effects of his treatment. Daniel should have seen it straight away. He'd watched his father suffer the same thing.

"Should he even be here?"

Muriel puffed out her chest again. "Absolutely. He's been looking forward to this for weeks. The cancer hasn't held him down at all. Terry has worked all the way through his treatment. He wrote new chapters for his book, recorded his album. He's been on TV and no one noticed. You know what Terry is like. The worst thing he could do is show weakness."

She was right. Terry was old-school. The show would always go on for him. "Okay." He sighed.

"And you can't let him suspect that you know," she insisted. "Just pretend everything is normal and let Terry do his thing. He's a survivor. Let him prove it."

* * * *

"Brandy," Max insisted. "For everyone. Let's round this meal off in style. Bring us a bottle of your finest cognac. It's my treat, I insist."

They'd already consumed a fair measure of alcohol around the table. Elijah was surprised, especially at Daniel, Max and Terry, who all had to sing tomorrow.

Most singers were strict about protecting their voices before a big show. But he knew it wouldn't matter. They would deliver their best and the audience wouldn't notice. They were professionals, but tonight they needed to let their hair down.

Daniel more than anyone. Elijah didn't know what was wrong, but he was uptight about something. He'd been in a peculiar mood ever since they arrived, getting worse as the evening wore on. He put on a big show, telling funny stories, laughing at other people's jokes, praising every mouthful of food. Elijah could see it was an act.

Something had rattled him. Maybe another call from Keeley when he had gone to use the bathroom. Whatever it was, he had a stick up his arse.

Everyone else was on fine form. Even Joe had relaxed and joined in with the group once he put his phone away.

At the end of the meal, Josh, the owner, returned to the table.

"How was everything?" he asked.

"Perfect," Elijah told him. "Everything has been first-rate. The food, the wine, the service. We've had the best time."

Josh smiled, looking proud. "That's always good to hear."

Josh seemed rather young and sure of himself to be overseeing such a great restaurant. He certainly had confidence. Elijah wondered whether he had a business partner—even more so, whether he would like one. Why not? He could learn a lot from a guy like Josh, he wasn't ready to go into the restaurant business on his own. He needed a partner.

Would Josh be interested?

The thought was appealing.

But tonight wasn't the time or the place to find out. They had too many other things going on right now. He filed the idea away. Maybe, in a day or two, if he still felt the same, he would give Josh a call.

* * * *

At one a.m. the beach was deserted and black. The sea smashed against a rocky outcrop somewhere in the inky darkness. The woman stared from the window of the holiday cottage but saw nothing. Her focus was inward.

It was almost over. So close, she could taste victory. A sweetness to be savored.

In a few more hours, her son would be avenged.

His murderers punished.

If she'd been looking at her reflection in the window, she would have seen the fleeting suggestion of a smile, but she saw nothing but the pictures in her mind.

Daniel Blake. Dead at last. A moment to be savored.

Outside, the waves continued to break.

Chapter Thirteen

Daniel woke the next morning with a rough head. The mother of all hangovers. Damn. Of all the days for this to happen. Still, the booze had allowed him a full night's sleep, something he hadn't expected. He'd had too much on his mind last night — today's rehearsals and the show, Keeley's detour to Blackpool and the news about Terry — to get a good night's sleep. But thanks to all that wine and brandy, he went out as soon as he lay down.

For that small mercy, he'd cope with the aftereffect.

The steady breath on the pillow behind him meant Elijah was still asleep. Daniel slid from the covers and picked his way through the debris of clothes to the bathroom. He took two paracetamol and stretched his aching back until his morning erection dwindled enough to take a piss.

Through the opaque glass of the bathroom window, the morning looked gray. In the bedroom, he parted the lined curtains to take in the view. Their room faced seaward, which this morning was an undulating mass of white-tipped waves. Rain dribbled down the pane.

"What time is it?" Elijah asked from the bed.

"About half-eight," Daniel said. "It looks pretty drab outside. What's the forecast for today?"

"Not sure." Elijah flicked on the bedside light and sat up, repositioning the pillows behind his head. His dark hair stuck up in tufts and twists. Daniel loved his disheveled appearance first thing in the morning. Elijah grabbed his phone and tapped the screen. "Doesn't look good. Rain. Getting worse as the day goes on. Winds picking up later."

"That sucks," Daniel said, slipping back into bed and pressing his naked body against Elijah's hot flesh.

"Hmm." Elijah frowned at the screen. "Potential storms this evening."

"So what else is new?" Daniel asked, snuggling farther in. "I always seem to be performing in a storm."

Elijah chuckled, putting the phone down. He shifted onto his side and casually put his hand on Daniel's hip. Firm, warm, welcome. "You should write a song about that. Or make it the name of your next album. Daniel Blake — *Performing Through the Storm*."

He chuckled. "When it comes to album titles, Terry's *Glitter Balls* will take some beating."

"He's got you there. I don't think you can top that one."

"I won't try," he said, hiding a pang of sadness.

Poor Terry. Bravely trying to maintain the façade of showbiz glamor while going through so much treatment.

"What's wrong?" Elijah asked, moving his hand across Daniel's waist to his ribcage.

"Nothing. Nerves about this evening, that's all."

"C'mon, it's me you're talking to. You don't get nervous about gigs like this. You can do them blindfolded with both hands tied behind your back. You were in a strange mood all last night. What's bugging you?"

In the bleak light of the bedroom, Elijah's deep brown eyes still had the capacity to draw him in. "Trust me," Daniel said, "it's nothing to do with either of us."

"Babe, it's got to be something to eat you up like this. If you don't tell me, I'll go out of my mind with worry."

"All right," he said, sliding his legs in between Elijah's. "But you can't breathe a word of this. I'm not supposed to know myself."

"My lips are sealed."

He told him about his conversation with Muriel. "Terry will have a shit-fit if he finds out she's told me. For her sake, we have to keep it quiet."

"The old girl thinks the world of Terry. I don't know how she puts up with him, but she does. If she says it's for the best, we must go with that. She knows him better than anyone."

"I know. It just feels so helpless, that's all."

Elijah moved closer, wrapping his arms around him. Daniel embraced him gratefully, pushing his body along his warm length.

"You're not helpless," Elijah said, nuzzling the side of Daniel's face. "Neither is Terry. He's a trooper. If he wants to do his show tonight, the best thing you can do is let him."

"I know. You're right. It's just so sad, that's all."

"The man is putting on a show while undergoing treatment for cancer. There's nothing sad about that. He's amazing."

When Daniel first met Terry on the *Anthem*, he would have been happy if he'd never seen the old guy again. For those first two days, he'd been a nightmare. A real pain in the arse. Catty and bitchy, he had made snide remarks or passed dirty looks whenever they came across each other. That had all changed on the third day. When Anouska Frost went missing. Terry was the first member of the crew to show any concern. By the time her absence was taken seriously, it was already too late. None of them knew that then, and Terry's determination to find her was what saved Daniel's life.

He wished he could do something to help Terry now.

He dove deep into Elijah's arms, lying still and quiet, inhaling the comforting scent of his chest hair. What a pity they had so many things to deal with today. He would rather stay here and block the world out. All its complications and sadness. Just pull the covers over their heads and ignore it all.

Fuck that, he thought after a moment. They'd come here for a reason, a fine one. To feed people, entertain them and make a heap of money for a worthy cause. *You can't do it lying here, feeling sorry for yourself.*

"C'mon," he said. "Let's get moving. The kisses and cuddles can wait until tonight."

Elijah slipped his hands over Daniel's hip and groped his arse. "Is that a promise?" he asked, squeezing flesh.

Daniel perked up. Since Friday, all Elijah wanted to do was get fucked. Was he ready to flip things over again? "I don't need to make those kinds of promises," Daniel told him. "It's all yours, any time you want it."

Elijah kissed him on the lips. "That's all I need to hear. Let's get this show on the road, so I can get back here to make good on your comments."

Daniel rolled onto his back, revealing how turned on Elijah had got him. His cock was up hard. "What do you want me to do with this?"

"Save it," Elijah said, hurling the bedclothes to the floor. "We've both got too much to do."

"Spoilsport." He pouted.

"Oh, I'll be worth the wait," he said, padding naked across the room. "Unlike my slow roast lamb if I don't get it in the oven soon."

After two years together, Daniel hadn't got tired of Elijah's arse. The sight of him walking away, buttocks jiggling, was insanely hot. As sexy as sin itself.

When Elijah turned on the shower, Daniel knew there'd be no chance of diverting him. Just as well. They did have a lot to do today. Why did hangovers have to make him so horny?

He got out of bed and took a bottle of water from the minibar, then downed it in one go. By the time he'd finished, his hard-on had subsided. Fun times with Elijah could wait until later. If they weren't too tired after all that work.

Too tired to have sex with Elijah? That would never be an issue.

Certainly not this side of their sixties, and maybe not even then. He intended to enjoy a very long, very happy sex life.

His thoughts were cut short by a knock at the door.

"Yeah?" he called, foraging for his underpants. They were beside the bed where he'd kicked them off last night.

"It's Joe."

Daniel pulled on his snug briefs and answered the door. No need for modesty around the boy. Joe had been his dresser for three months in Blackpool. He'd seen it all before. No point being coy around him now.

"Can I have the car keys?" Joe asked, sweeping past, taking no notice of Daniel's near-naked state.

In turn, Daniel was startled by the change in Joe's demeanor. He had styled his hair into the familiar quaff he used to wear and had ditched the somber wardrobe for a striped blue polo shirt and a pair of shorts. The luster in his olive-gray eyes was radiant. If he wasn't so thin, he could pass for the boy Daniel used to know.

"You look good," he told him.

"You look…underdressed," Joe said cheekily.

"Won't you be early?" Daniel asked, fetching the car keys from his jacket in the wardrobe.

"Better than being late."

The pungent scent of Joe's aftershave filled the bedroom. He must be wearing a whole bottle. Daniel took a credit card from his wallet and wrote his PIN on a slip of hotel notepaper. "Take this," he said, putting both in Joe's hand.

"No, Daniel, I can't," he said, staring at the card. "You don't have to."

"I want to," he insisted. "To make up for being so sulky with you last night. I was in a funny mood and feel rotten about it now. So, lunch, for you and Callum."

"But we're eating tonight," Joe protested.

"Tonight is dinner. This is lunch. I'm buying. Two growing lads like you don't need to worry about your waistlines. Take Callum somewhere nice and enjoy it. You deserve it."

Joe threw his arms around him. Daniel concealed the shock he felt embracing his skeletal frame. Joe's ribs were clearly discernible beneath his fingers. Jesus, there was nothing on him.

But this morning gave the first hint that Joe had turned a corner. His smile was genuine, it radiated from his mouth and his eyes. God knows he had a long way to go, but at last he appeared to be moving in the right direction.

* * * *

Joe got lost twice trying to find his way to Durham. Despite directions from the satnav, the roads around the hotel all looked the same. With steep fields and meadows on either side, and most of the road signs concealed behind overgrown hedges, they looped and wound without a single landmark to get his bearings by. Callum was already waiting when Joe arrived at the station on top of another hill.

He leaned against the wall with an overnight bag at his feet, looking gorgeous in shorts, flip-flops and an open-neck polo shirt. His tight torso and hairy limbs caused a stirring in Joe's pants. Joe pulled up at the curb and wound down the window.

"Sorry I'm late," he said breathlessly.

Callum flashed a million-dollar smile before taking in the car. "Whoa. Is this yours?"

"I wish. It's Daniel's. Get in, I've only got it on loan for an hour or so."

"Cool."

The fresh, sexy scent of Callum's cologne filled the car, as he slid onto the passenger seat. Without hesitating, he leaned over, put a hand on the back of Joe's head and drew him into a kiss. Joe didn't resist.

He surrendered to Callum's confident lips, thrilled by the roughness of his dark stubble.

"Missed you," Callum said, breaking free, sexy smile spread wide.

"Me too," Joe replied. The words made him strangely self-conscious, exposed, though they were true. He fought the sensation. Hating this shyness. Maybe some of Callum's confidence would rub off on him in time. He hoped so.

"What's the plan?" Callum asked, fastening his seat belt. "I can't wait to meet your friends."

What Joe really wanted to do was drive straight back to the hotel. He had a massive double room with a deluxe bed that they should take advantage of. But it would be too forward to suggest that straightaway. Instead he said, "How about a look around the city first? I've never been before and, you being a local boy, I thought you could give me a tour."

"Okay," Callum said, without much enthusiasm. "Though this is a small place. More like a modest town. Let's head down to the center and take a look around."

Callum directed him to a car park on the other side of the river, right on the waterfront, and they walked up into the small city center, which was an ancient marketplace, with cobbled streets and old monuments. Pretty, but Joe soon realized he was in no mood for sightseeing. He found Callum far more attractive than the historic buildings. There was a stall in the center of the square, selling ice creams. Callum bought them a cone each and insisted on paying.

Though the sky was a deathly shade of gray, the earlier rain had subsided and it was an uncomfortably warm and muggy afternoon. Even in shorts, Joe felt clammy and prickly, though the ice cream went some way to cooling him down.

"What do you want to see?" Callum asked, licking his lips. "The cathedral, the castle, a museum?"

God no. Joe didn't want to see any of those fusty things. "Maybe it's a bit too hot for that," he said.

"Yeah, and boring." He laughed. "I was only trying to impress you with how clever I was. Thank God you said no."

"Daniel wants us to have lunch. It's on him," Joe said. "Maybe we can just go for a walk before finding somewhere to eat."

Callum raised both eyebrows. "Daniel Blake? What? He's buying lunch?"

Joe nodded. "He insisted."

"Wow. That's so cool. Is he meeting us here?"

"No. Daniel's not coming. He's rehearsing his show. But he gave me his card to buy lunch."

"He must be a great guy."

"He is. The best. Daniel and Elijah are both amazing."

Callum shook his head, laughing. "Man, this is unreal. I can't believe you're best friends with Daniel Blake. I've always wanted to meet him. Not just that, but he's paying for lunch. It's unreal."

"He's just a regular guy. Don't expect him to act like a big star or anything. That's not the way he is."

"Is he sexy?"

"What?"

"I mean in reality. He's so hot when you see him on TV and in magazines, but not all guys are the same when you see them for real. We had a couple of guys from *Emmerdale* in the restaurant last week. I always thought they were gorgeous in the show, but they're nothing special in person. And short. Really short."

"Daniel's not short," Joe said tartly. "He's my friend, I don't look at him like that."

"Oh, c'mon. Daniel Blake, are you kidding? You must look at him. He's soooo good-looking. Like perfect. He's one of the first guys I ever had a crush on."

Joe looked away, no longer comfortable with the way Callum stared at him. He searched for a rubbish bin to get rid of his ice-cream cone. He'd had enough.

"C'mon," Callum continued eagerly. "Tell me about him."

Joe stood and crossed to a waste bin. Callum was right behind him. Why was he acting like a dick all of a sudden? He'd not indicated he was such a Daniel Blake fan until now. "Is that the only reason you came?" he asked, turning to glare at him. "To meet Daniel. 'Cause he won't appreciate it. Daniel is with Elijah. He wouldn't look twice at anyone else. Neither of them would."

The bright smile faded. Callum stepped closer. "Babe, of course not. I'm here because of you."

"So why are you banging on about Daniel?"

"I'm excited, that's all. This might be nothing to you—you're friends with these guys, fancy dos like tonight are probably a regular thing for you—but it's a big deal to a guy like me. I don't mix in celebrity circles. But I came because of you." He moved closer and put his hands around Joe's waist, pulling their hips together. He touched his forehead to Joe's. "I'm sorry. I didn't mean to sound like a douche. I get star-struck, that's all."

Joe stood stiff in his hold and stared anxiously around. No one paid them any attention, and yet, this made him uncomfortable. The dreaded tightness that signaled the start of a panic attack gripped his chest. He broke away and took a step back. Callum came toward him again with open arms. Joe held him back. "Just…easy. Not here. I don't like it."

Callum's smile returned, full wattage. "No one cares about us. Look, no one is watching."

"I care." He took a deep breath, getting his nerves under control.

"Okay. I get it. And I am sorry. Can we start again?"

Slow breaths. In and out. The strain eased. Finally, he nodded.

"C'mon then, let's take that walk before lunch. I know a great path along the side of the river."

Something had stiffened in Joe's legs. The first couple of steps were difficult. He fought it. He could do this. He wouldn't be beaten. "All right," he said, following Callum across the square. "That sounds nice."

* * * *

By early afternoon, Elijah's confidence had grown. Pulling off the menu was a big ask, but he was getting there. Working side by side with hotel chef, Magda, and her kitchen assistants, Pearl and Arif, everything had gone to plan. The lamb, potatoes and carrots for his main course were already in the ovens at a low heat. They would stay there for the rest of the day until the meat was tender and fell from the bone, and the vegetables absorbed all the delicious roasting juices. Consulting his checklist and ticking off another two tasks, Elijah allowed himself a moment to catch his breath. They could do this. They were doing this.

"Why don't you take a half-hour break," he said to Pearl and Arif. They were students from a local catering college and had worked hard and enthusiastically all morning. The preparations were ahead of schedule. They deserved a breather.

"Twenty-minutes," Magda told them sternly.

"Really?" Elijah asked her when they had left.

"I tell them twenty minutes, they'll be back in half an hour. You tell them half an hour, they'll take three-quarters. It's the golden rule of running a kitchen, always keep on top of the staff. Cut them no slack."

He didn't doubt her. Magda was an imposing woman. In her early fifties, she had a broad, humorless face and huge, muscular forearms. When he met her yesterday, he'd been awed at having to tell her what to do, but even then, Magda was resolute. "This is your evening and your menu. You're in charge. I'm only here to help you achieve that."

The facilities were second to none but without her guidance he'd have no idea of how to operate any of the equipment. It was so different from his kitchen at home, or Kostas' restaurant in Corfu. Magda had ordered all the ingredients based on the menu and numbers of guests he'd provided. The quality of her supplies was superb. Without a doubt, Elijah knew this would be one special meal.

Magda fished inside her trouser pockets and produced a packet of cigarettes. "I'm going outside. Want one?"

"No thanks. I don't smoke. I'll just see how things are going in the hall."

In the main reception, he spotted a couple of security officers carrying out an assessment of the venue. A year ago, he wouldn't have given security a second thought, especially for a charity function like this. Now it was top of the agenda, above the food and the music. When he'd first discussed plans for the gala with April, he'd stressed to her that safety was more important than anything. No one would be allowed in without a ticket, and all bags and jackets would be searched at the door. There would be two undercover guards in the main hall all evening and another two on the front door. All staff working in the hotel had been vetted in advance. Nothing left to chance. No fuck ups. Not this time.

"Everything going okay?" he asked, approaching the guards and introducing himself.

"Nothing to worry about," the older of the men said with confidence. "We've checked the hotel CCTV system and all the public areas. We'll have additional staff on the main gate this evening. No one gets access to the grounds unless they're on the guest list. In addition to bag searches at the front door, we've also brought a metal detector. Everyone coming through the door will be scanned head to toe."

"Good."

A lot of the guests wouldn't like it. Many would object. Tough. If they wanted in, they'd have to suck it up. No exceptions.

This was how it must be.

The world was a dangerous place. Their world more than others.

Elijah could take no chances. Not this time.

Chapter Fourteen

The clouds over Rockcliffe Manor had thickened and darkened as the afternoon drew on, blackening the sky, until finally, around six o'clock, the storm they had threatened broke, unleashing a torrential downpour on the guests arriving for the gala. Ladies in fine and expensive gowns were escorted from their cars beneath golf umbrellas borrowed from the club.

From the first-floor green room at the front of the house, Daniel and Max watched the procession of vehicles from the main gate, followed by the hasty rush of well-dressed guests to the main door.

"What a shame," Daniel said, as he saw two women in cocktail dresses rush for the entrance without the aid of an umbrella, trying and failing to preserve their hairstyles. "Why couldn't it have held off another half-hour?"

"Typical British weather," she said. "I wouldn't go as far as my front gate without a brolly. You never know when it will turn. Besides, we didn't promise the sunshine with those tickets. Just a good dinner and a show. On that front, we can deliver."

On arrival, the guests were received with canapés and cocktails before being ushered into the hall. The schedule for the evening was tight. Terry was up first at seven thirty, followed by Max at eight. Dinner would be served from eight thirty, during which they would host an auction, then Daniel would perform his headline set at ten thirty. From eleven thirty onward, Ben would take over the DJ booth until the curfew on the bar at one. Everyone knew what they had to do and when. It should be a great night.

And one that would raise a lot of money. They'd already taken a bundle on ticket sales, but Daniel predicted the auction to be the real moneymaker. He'd work his arse off to ensure it was.

The rain rattled more persistently on the window.

They'd all have to try extra hard to raise the spirits of the damp crowd.

Max drew him away. "Let's have a little drink. For the old nerves."

They were the only two in the green room. Terry was already downstairs, preparing his show, while Elijah was in the kitchen and April was playing hostess. At some point he expected her to appear with a handful of local dignitaries and VIPs. This room was set up for their benefit rather than the entertainers, but at the moment, it was the quietest place in the hotel. Daniel and Max took full advantage.

"Where's Ben?"

"Still in the bath when I left. You men, I swear you take far longer than us girls to get dressed."

"I doubt he's been in the beauty parlor all afternoon, unlike some people," he teased.

"Oh, darling. I needed it. All that sun and sea air has played havoc with my skin. I needed a little touch-up before anyone saw me."

"You look amazing, as always."

"Thank you, darling. What are you drinking?"

"Make it a small whiskey."

"Ice? Water?"

"Just water."

Max was already dressed for the stage in a sheer floor-length gown, encrusted with thousands of golden crystals. Her sun-kissed hair fell in soft waves to her shoulders. She was barefoot. Her huge strappy heels lay on the floor beside her handbag, ready to put on before she left. She handed him the drink and poured the same for herself.

"Cheers," he said, raising his glass.

"Cheers." They clinked. "Hey, where's the poisoned dwarf? Isn't she coming? I haven't seen her yet."

"Shit, yes." He'd been so tied up getting ready for this evening, he'd forgotten all about Keeley. He'd tried to call her after breakfast with no success. After that he'd forgotten about her. He snatched the phone and called reception to see if she'd checked in.

"No, sir. Not yet."

"As soon as she arrives, can you let me know?"

"Probably another wild goose chase," Max said. "I bet the silly cow has gotten herself lost. You know what those London-based journos are like as soon they get north of the M25. If we're lucky, she won't get here until after dinner. I'm not sure I could eat with her in my face."

"You're too hard on her. Keeley isn't that bad."

Max screwed her face. "You keep telling me that, but I don't believe you."

"Give her a chance."

"Just keep the two of us apart and everything will go fantastically well."

"Somehow, I doubt that."

* * * *

Where in the bastard depths of hell am I?

Torrential rain smacked the windscreen of Keeley's car, reducing visibility to little more than a few yards ahead of the hood. Which would be bad enough even if these roads weren't so narrow and winding. Her tight hands, gripping the wheel, began to cramp. She slowly released and stretched each digit, easing some of the strain. *Damn the fucking countryside. How can anyone stand it out here in this shithole?*

When she'd checked the map for her route from Blackpool to Durham, the obvious, easiest way would have been to stay on the motorway, cutting across through Harrogate to the A1, then following the road north. But as she set off, the satnav recalculated the route, finding a quicker way that would save a good hour. Great idea. The sooner she got there, the better. She'd been unable to reach Daniel on the phone for a whole day now and needed to speak to him urgently. Before he went on that bloody stage tonight.

The sky was already dimming, and it would be night soon. How much farther did she have to go?

The display on her route planner read sixty-six miles. One hour and twenty minutes.

Fuck! She'd been on the road for two hours already. *Some fucking shortcut this has turned out to be.*

She saw a sign ahead. Kirby Stephen, 1 mile.

Where do they get these ridiculous place names?

Keeley sped up. There looked to be a town coming up. Maybe it would mean an end to these awful back roads.

Around the next bend, she unexpectedly found a car coming straight at her. With a shriek, she realized she had drifted onto the wrong side of the road. He wrenched the wheel to the left and the back end of her vehicle slewed as she tried to get back to her own lane. The other car compensated and passed her with a screaming blare on their horn.

"Fuckwit," she screamed, getting under control. These roads were so narrow, it was a wonder there weren't more accidents.

If she made it in one piece, she would stick to motorways from now on.

No more fucking shortcuts.

* * * *

Terry's show kicked off on time. No one could afford to be late. With the schedule so tight, everything had to run like clockwork. Most of the guests were seated at their tables when he began. Outside, the weather had deteriorated, but, for the next few hours, no one would care about that.

Daniel watched from the side of the stage. Terry seemed in significant pain as he took his seat at the piano, wincing as he arranged himself. Muriel placed a large glass of something in front of him and he knocked most of it off in a single draught. When the lights went up, and he began to play, it was as if a switch had tripped. Terry sat up, spine perfectly straight, with a wide smile plastered across his face, and launched into his opening number. The applause was rapturous, with several people whooping their appreciation. Terry nodded and mouthed a thank-you between lines.

His voice was awful, but that was nothing new. Even at his peak, Terry used to talk more of the lyrics than he sang. Nobody cared. It was entertainment, and he knew how to deliver it. It was something that couldn't be taught, the ability to get an audience on side despite his obvious limitations. Terry made it look effortless. Rehearsals this afternoon had not been good, and Daniel had worried about his ability to pull off the short, thirty-minute set. His concerns were groundless. Given a crowd, Terry could always deliver.

No one commented on how delicate he looked. Maybe they hadn't noticed. He knew how different people could look in real life compared to how they appeared on TV.

Toward the end of the set, showing no signs of flagging, Terry called Daniel onto the stage with him. The audience went even crazier. No one expected this. It was a last-minute addition to the show this afternoon.

"Welcome my dear friend Daniel," Terry told the crowd. "You might not believe this, but we have never sung together on stage before. Max LaFranchi had the honor of performing with him every night in the show *Lady Lynda*. Well, as wonderful as Max is, I couldn't let her get one over on me. I might not get an opportunity like this again, I couldn't let it pass. So, for the first time ever...and hopefully not the last, a duet with Daniel Blake."

Daniel struggled to hear the music as Terry started the song — the applause was near deafening. The orchestra struck up behind him, giving it some base. Grinning, he took his position at the side of the piano while Terry beamed at him from the seat. The song was

Younger Than Springtime from *South Pacific*. Not usually performed as a duet, but they'd come up with an arrangement that allowed Terry to sing-talk his lines while Daniel belted out the big notes.

A rush of emotion surged through Daniel as he sang, threatening to engulf him. This couldn't be a one-time deal. He wouldn't allow it. He had to sing with Terry again before it got too late. Maybe bring him in to do something on his album. He wouldn't let it turn into a moment of regret. Tears prickled his eyelids at the end of the song. He blinked them away before helping Terry to his feet. The older man leaned on him as they took a bow, then against the piano as Daniel stepped aside so he could enjoy the applause for himself.

He deserved it.

"Thank you," Terry whispered afterward, clutching his hand as he supported him off the stage. "That was wonderful."

"It was. Thanks for asking me to do it," he said, hugging him in return, careful not to squeeze too tight.

* * * *

"Oh, man, he is so hot," Callum exclaimed as Daniel left the stage. "I always thought he would be, but, God, the TV and magazines do not do him justice. I can't believe how handsome he is."

"All right." Joe sighed. "I get it. You don't have to keep going on about it. Daniel is hot."

"Sorry," Callum said, not taking his eyes off Daniel. Following him as he led Terry down the steps and off through the curtain. Only then did he turn to look at Joe. "I know I'm raving. I'm star-struck, that's all."

Callum was looking pretty himself. His dark hair, delicious eyes and chiseled features worked a treat in his rented tuxedo. But the constant questions and remarks about Daniel were a major pain. "I don't know why. You told me you get celebrities in the restaurant all the time."

"We do. But come on, this is Daniel Blake. The man is stunning. Even you must be able to admit that."

Joe reached for his drink, a cold glass of wine, and knocked it off. A waitress appeared and filled it back to the top. She'd been doing that ever since they'd sat down, and he had no idea how much he'd drunk. Maybe a bottle already. He grabbed his water glass and downed that too. It wouldn't do to get drunk and embarrass himself. Callum was on track to do a pretty good job of that already. Bringing him along had been a major mistake.

It proved to Joe how you couldn't really know anyone after a couple of nights together and a few dozen texts.

It had been going so well too. Back in Leeds, Callum had been the perfect date. Funny, kind, intelligent, exceptionally well-hung—he'd had everything going for him. At least it had seemed as if he did. Even today, after his comments about Daniel in town, he'd calmed down. After lunch, they'd come back to the hotel and enjoyed a hot, passionate afternoon in Joe's bedroom. Callum knew all the right moves in bed. When his mouth was occupied, he was perfect boyfriend material.

But the questions had started again when they'd started getting ready for the gala. He'd sat on the toilet and reeled them out the whole time Joe had been in the shower. *Tell me more about Daniel. How long did you work for him? Did you ever see him naked in his dressing room? Did he ever make a move on you?*

Totally inappropriate and he knew the answers to most of them already. Anyone with a computer could find out what Joe was doing in Daniel's room in Blackpool. And Callum had done his research. He probably knew more about Daniel than even Elijah. He was starting to sound obsessed.

He wouldn't shut up.

Max LaFranchi came on stage right after Terry, shimmying to the front in a sparkling dress. "How on earth am I going to follow that?" she said, grinning at the crowd.

"You can't," Callum muttered as everyone else applauded. "Stupid old has-been."

Joe shot him a look. *What the fuck am I doing with this loser? I've fallen for the first good-looking man to pay me some attention.* It could be worse, he reasoned. Callum had shown his true colors early. Joe wouldn't have to waste six months dating him before the mask slipped.

He wouldn't cause a scene. Not tonight. But when this was over, he'd be sure to lose Callum's number. For good.

Max launched into *Roses and Rainbows*, her big number. Everyone knew it. Around the room people got to their feet and headed for the dance floor.

"Actually, I quite like this one," Callum said. "Want to dance?"

"No," Joe said. "I want a cigarette." He got up and hurried to the door without looking back.

* * * *

"I could do with a few minutes to catch my breath," Terry said, once they were backstage, out of the glare of the crowd. The moment he stepped from the spotlight, the persona he'd created for the audience disappeared, like blowing out a match. His bony fingers held Daniel's elbow tight, and his makeup looked like a wax mask sitting on top of his skin.

Daniel guided him to a chair and Terry sat with some visible relief. Daniel poured him a glass from a jug of iced water. "Sip it slowly," he cautioned, handing him the glass.

"Wasn't that wonderful?" The smile took an effort. Terry's hands trembled as he brought the water to his lips.

"They love you," Daniel said, crouching to meet Terry's eyes. "Are you okay?"

"Absolutely." He was out of breath. "It's the adrenaline of a performance, that's all. Don't worry about me, you've got enough to do tonight."

"I am worried about you," Daniel said, squeezing his knee. "Why don't you go for a lie-down. You've done your part."

"I couldn't possibly. I've been looking forward to this evening for months. I don't want to miss a thing."

At that moment, Muriel appeared. Her face clouded at the sight of Terry. "Why don't we go to the room for a little while?" She spoke in her usual crisp, businesslike manner, putting on a front. Daniel realized that Terry's entire life was a front, and the best thing they could do for him was join in the façade. "We can come back down in a little while, eh? Maybe skip some of the meal and join in for the dessert?"

"Oh well." Terry took another shaky sip of water. "To tell the truth, I'm not very hungry. It would be a waste of good food. It's not a bad idea, I suppose. Do you think Elijah would mind too much if I sat out the first couple of courses?"

"Don't be daft," Daniel answered brightly. "It'll mean less work for him."

Terry nodded, and looked relieved. "Okay. I'll take that rest and see you in an hour or so." He raised his hand, gesturing for them to help him up.

"Do you want me to come with you?" Daniel asked once Terry was on his feet.

"It's okay," Muriel said, "I can take care of this. Go back to the party."

"Yes, stop fussing. I'm not dead yet. Far from it. Get out there and give those people what they came for. God knows, they've paid enough for it."

With a noticeable effort Terry pulled himself straight. Linking arms with Muriel, he treated Daniel to another of his wide smiles, before walking away.

Daniel kept his own smile fixed and rigid until they were gone. Then everything dropped. He sat in the chair Terry had just vacated and took a deep breath. *Shit.* The old man was in a far worse state than he'd imagined. He didn't care what Muriel said about keeping quiet, or Terry's old-fashioned sense of pride. Tomorrow morning, he'd get Terry to tell him exactly what was happening. He wanted to know the kind of treatment he was having and what was being done for his pain because he was in a huge amount of discomfort.

The performance he'd just given couldn't have helped.

Daniel just hoped it hadn't made things worse.

* * * *

In the main hall of Rockcliffe Manor, excitement reached a palpable level.

Max LaFranchi had delivered a first-rate act. The whole room was in agreement.

"As good as anything I've seen in Vegas," one man declared.

"No," another on his table disagreed. "She was better than Vegas."

Their enthusiasm was shared around the room. Terry and Max had knocked it out of the park and the evening had only begun. The meal was still to come, followed by the headline performance from Daniel. Everyone agreed this was a special night indeed.

One woman kept her distance, watching and listening. It would be a special night all right, but not for the reasons these idiots believed.

They had better make the most of Daniel Blake's performance.

Because they were about to hear the last songs he would ever sing.

Chapter Fifteen

With the main course served, Elijah had his first moment of calm all evening. The desserts were prepared and in the fridge, ready for plating up. The hard work was done.

"Great job, everyone," he told the small kitchen team. It was a miracle. That a handful of people could achieve all that.

"It's not over yet," Magda told her team in a stern voice. "Clean down and get ready for service on the sweets."

He patted her on the shoulder. "Five minutes." He thought the kids deserved a short break. They'd all worked hard. Though this was Magda's kitchen, technically he was in charge tonight. "They're going to do the auction before we serve dessert."

Elijah took a bottle of water from the fridge and drank down the whole thing. He was on fire. The last three hours had been a super-fast blur. He thought he'd probably enjoyed it, but it was too soon to know, he struggled to remember any of the things he'd done. All he knew for certain was that he wanted to do it again. He grabbed a wad of paper towels and wiped his brow and neck. The hair at the back of his head was soaking wet.

There was a huge boom of thunder right over the hotel, followed by a monstrous crack of lightning. He knew it had been raining hard throughout service, but had no idea the storm had moved above them. He went to the kitchen door and opened it. The sudden burst of cooler air into the hot kitchen was a relief, though, outside, the rain hit the ground so hard it bounced back a foot into the air.

Elijah hadn't seen a storm like this in a long time. Not since...that last night on the *Anthem*. Searching the decks of the ship for Anouska during an Atlantic squall. He shivered at the memory. That evening had also started as a night of celebration, just like this. How soon it had turned to shit. *Stop it.* He refused to relive that horror again.

There was nothing to fear here.

"Elijah."

He jumped at the sound of his name. *Why so nervous all of a sudden?*

Joe stood behind him. "Hey, are you all right? You look like you've seen a ghost."

He shook his head and shrugged. "I'm fine, I guess my nerves are a little frazzled. It's been an intense few hours."

"I don't doubt that." Joe grinned. "That meal was immense. Really. I don't even like lamb that much, but I loved it. And the potatoes you served with it. Sooo good."

Elijah hoped the boy was telling the truth and not just flattering him. The image of Joe pushing food around his plate without eating was hard to shake. He'd witnessed it twice in the last few days. "I hope you saved room for dessert."

"Seeing as it's you, I'll make room. But they need you in the hall first. The auction has started. They want to announce your lot before they open the bids."

"Shit. I totally forgot about that." Glancing down at his chef's whites, splattered with grease and sauce, he realized he couldn't go out like that. "Magda, are there any spare tunics?"

With an unlit cigarette in her mouth and an umbrella in her hand, Magda jerked her head toward the pantry. Elijah found one in his size and quickly changed into it.

Daniel and Max were on the stage when he came into the hall through a side door. April worked the floor with a handheld microphone. The atmosphere struck him the second he entered. It was electric. Daniel and Max were a great double act. Sparring off each other, joking with the crowd, they loved being on stage and it showed. Their enthusiasm was infectious.

Max spotted him first.

"Ladies and gentlemen," she announced with grandeur, "I hope you've saved your biggest cheer for the man who created the fabulous menu you've just enjoyed. You've feasted your appetite, now get ready to feast your eyes, because he's as beautiful as the food he cooks. Make some noise for the gorgeous Elijah Mann."

The applause was resounding as he made his way to the stage. He saw a blur of faces as people stood to shake his hand, pat his shoulder, praise and congratulate him. Smiling, a little embarrassed, he made it to the front and joined the others. It was bright up there, too bright. *Boy, am I out of practice.* Elijah had not been on stage in a long time. It used to come so naturally to him. Working the crowd, being the center of attention. He was a stranger to it now. An alien.

Max embraced him with a double air kiss before Daniel came in for a stronger hug. Elijah clung to him, reassuring and familiar. "You're gonna have to help me out," Elijah whispered.

Daniel leaned back, looking at him quizzically.

"I don't think I can do this anymore," Elijah mouthed.

Daniel gave a short nod of understanding, before turning to the audience, mega-watt smile in place, keeping the microphone to himself, his other arm on Elijah's shoulder.

"You all enjoyed the food tonight, yes? Yes?" The answer was an astounding certainty. "That's a relief. Because I know how much time, effort, care and attention Elijah put into this dinner. It's no exaggeration to say he's been planning this for weeks, no, months. He used to be at home here on the stage with Max and myself, but now he's more at home in the kitchen, and I'm sure everyone will agree that comedy's loss is a culinary gain."

Elijah put a hand around Daniel's waist and squeezed, showing his gratitude.

Stage fright had never been an obstacle for him. In the early days of his career, playing to hostile crowds in comedy clubs, he was never disheartened. He saw it as a challenge. To win the audience over and make them laugh, bringing them onside. That drive, that need to be in the spotlight, he didn't have it anymore. This wasn't his place. Like returning to a favorite bar or town and finding that everything had changed, that he no longer belonged.

Max, picking up on his reluctance to talk, continued with the auction. "If you enjoyed tonight's food, you're going to be knocked out by our next lot. This gorgeous man is offering a once-in-a-lifetime opportunity. He'll come to the home of the lucky winner and cook for you. Right there in your own kitchen. A private dinner party for...how many people? Eight?"

"Ten." Elijah found his voice. "I'll work with the winner to create a special menu especially to their taste."

"So, a dinner party for ten, cooked in your own home, by the one and only Elijah Mann. That's the kind of event money can't buy. Except tonight it can. So dig deep, ladies and gentlemen. How about we start the bidding at fifty pounds per head? That's five hundred pounds opening bid. How cheap is that? Who wants it?"

If she hadn't been such a great singer and actress, Max would have made a first-rate auctioneer. She had the skill, warmth, charisma and enthusiasm to get the crowd on side and bidding big. In a few swift bids she had the price of his dinner party up to four thousand pounds and people were still raising their hands. The price went up in increments of two hundred and fifty pounds, then five hundred pounds. On the floor, April worked the tables, geeing up the bids until it was finally done at fourteen thousand five hundred pounds. Elijah had to shake his head to be sure he'd heard it right.

"Fourteen and a half thousand for a gourmet dinner cooked for you by Elijah," Max enthused. "Well done to our winner. I think you got yourself a bargain. That's a fantastic prize."

It's insane. Holy hell. How am I gonna make good on that?

Elijah waved at the winning bidder, mouthing a huge thank-you. His heart raced as he stepped to the edge of the stage. What a rush.

"Whoa, hold on, mister." Max grabbed his elbow and led him back toward Daniel. "Not so fast."

"I thought I was done," he said, playing up to the audience.

"You're far from done. Dessert will have to wait a few minutes longer. I don't think anyone will mind."

She gestured for Ben to come up and join them. Elijah caught the bemusement on his face as he rose from his seat and made his way to the front.

"What's this?" Elijah whispered to Daniel.

"No idea," he replied under his breath. "She's gone off script."

Ben's cheeky dimples were in place as he stood next to them.

"Do you know anything about this?" Elijah asked.

"Not a thing." His eyes were wide, his grin even wider.

"Aren't they beautiful?" Max declared. "Three extraordinarily gorgeous men."

The audience hollered their agreement.

"This is a setup." Daniel laughed over his mic.

"Indeed it is," Max said. "But a worthy one. So this next lot is mainly for the ladies in the house, but if any of the guys want to join in, feel free. All bids are welcome. This is a one-time-only deal. You'll never get this opportunity again so don't miss out. I'm giving one lucky winner the chance to kiss not just one hot guy, not even two, but three top-drawer hotties."

Elijah, Daniel and Ben all groaned in good humor. They'd been stitched up.

"All in a great cause," Max continued. "Shall we start the bids at one hundred pounds?"

All around the room, hands thrust into the air.

* * * *

The line of traffic stretched around the next twist in the road. Keeley hadn't moved in over an hour. Behind her, a line of cars snaked out of sight. On either side, there was nothing but blackness. Torrential rain pounded on the roof and, with the radio turned up to the max, she could barely hear it. Some shitty yokel station reported an accident up ahead. A multiple vehicle pileup.

"It could take some time to move," the newsreader announced.

She was never going to get there.

Fuck. Fuck. Fuck. Dammit.

She smashed her palm against the steering wheel. Her mobile phone had run out of juice half an hour ago and she didn't have an adapter that would charge it in the car. She'd never thought she'd need it. This was supposed to be a two-and-a-half-hour journey. She should have been there hours ago. Not that the damn phone had been any use. She hadn't had a decent signal since she'd gotten onto these godforsaken back roads.

The route planner claimed she had another thirty-three miles till she reached her destination. If she ever got moving again.

Fucking Durham.

The place was cursed. For her at least. She should have known things would go wrong when Daniel had told her where the gala was taking place. Why hold it there? Of all the fucking places he could have chosen.

Keeley had promised herself she would never go back, yet here she was, stuck in a traffic jam from hell, trying to reach the last place she ever wanted to go.

The Durham Strangler. A deranged serial killer. Keeley's involvement in the case, and the three books she subsequently wrote on the subject, had turned her from a gossip journalist into a bestselling author. A celebrity.

A brutal killer murdering young men in a picture postcard cathedral city — it had been the kind of case most true-life crime-writers only dreamt about. But Keeley didn't dream. She had been right there when the murders were happening. She had even been on the scene when they dragged a body from the river. She had seen her opportunity and grabbed it.

But how she hated the place.

Even more as the years passed. She'd written about it over and over. Given lectures, appeared on TV shows and radio call-ins. Her name was indelibly linked with that of the Durham Strangler.

But not for much longer. Oh no, she'd see to that.

Her intuition for a good story had not let her down.

She knew there was more to what happened with Daniel Blake and Oliver Gill than a bit of showbiz rivalry. The story was bigger than that. More dangerous. The murders in Blackpool last year had proved her instincts right. She'd been in the right place at the right time again, making her the perfect person to crack the case.

And now she had.

Oh, boy, had she.

She knew the identity of Oliver's mother. The piece of the puzzle that had eluded everyone. The family, the press, the cops had all failed, but Keeley Rank had the story.

And if she could get off this fucking road, she'd give her book a perfect conclusion.

* * * *

"I wish I could've afforded one of those kisses. I don't care about the other two, Daniel would be enough for me."

"You can't," Joe snapped.

Callum's comments were seriously starting to grate. He would not shut up.

The winning bid had been four thousand four hundred pounds. Almost four and a half grand for a quick peck on the lips from three men. Three very handsome men, but, boy, some people had cash to burn. All in a good cause. If they wanted to throw their money around, they might as well throw it toward Supporting Victims. Joe hadn't been keeping count, but the charity was set to make a fortune.

The thought was some consolation for having had to sit beside Callum and listen to him perv over Daniel all night. His behavior got worse the more he drank. No better than a randy teenager. An obnoxious randy teenager. Joe had no one to blame but himself. It had been his own idea to bring Callum along and he'd had to pull a favor from Daniel to secure him a seat at the sold-out table. What a waste.

Callum had gone from hero to zero in a few short hours. It wasn't a complete loss. Joe had learned something. That he was ready to get back out there, to meet new people and start dating. So, he'd drawn a dud with Callum—it didn't mean there weren't better men waiting to be found. Men worth the time and effort.

The dessert plates were cleared away and the waiting staff returned with pots of coffee and a selection of petits fours.

"What time is Daniel coming back on?" Callum asked, brandishing his empty wine glass for a top-up.

"Soon," Joe bit back. He wondered whether he should slip backstage and watch the show from there, leaving Callum on his own out front. He doubted his date would even notice his absence. Though God knows what he'd try if Joe left him here unsupervised. Something crazy, no doubt.

Yeah, like sneaking into Daniel's room and arranging himself on the bed for a ménage à trois.

Joe shuddered at the memory. Jesus, not that long ago he'd been the infatuated idiot he now sat beside. No, it wouldn't do to leave Callum on his own.

If he was sticking with him, he would have to fortify himself.

"I want a smoke before the show starts," he said. "Want to come with me?"

Callum shook his head. "I'll wait here," he shouted. Like most drunks, he'd lost control of his volume. "Don't wanna miss a thing."

"Okay. Don't go away. I won't be long."

As Joe stood, Callum turned to the woman sitting on his other side. "Have you heard Daniel sing live before?" he slurred.

Oh God. Let this end quickly.

Breaking up would be easy. He'd tell it to him straight in the morning. Joe was heading home to Blackpool in another few days. When he did, he'd be sure to lose Callum's number. And block him on social media. No reason this had to be anything more than it was. A fleeting, misjudged affair.

The rain had gotten worse since he came out for his last cigarette, belting on the entrance of the hotel. The official smoking area was a gazebo around the far side of the building. Joe looked at the rain, coming down in a slanting sheet, and questioned whether he needed a nicotine fix that bad. Maybe it was time to cut back. To quit the cigarettes as well as Callum.

One thing at a time. He wasn't made of steel.

Borrowing one of the golf umbrellas from the foyer, he set out into the night. The umbrella kept his head and shoulders dry, but offered no protection from the water bouncing up from the ground. He picked up speed and resolved to have at least two, maybe three cigarettes for all the trouble he'd taken.

Finally reaching the shelter of the gazebo, he shook off the rain.

"Whoa," he said, shuddering beneath an electric heater.

There was no one there. Of course not, no one else would be that stupid. It sure was time to quit.

He retrieved the packet and lighter from his inside pocket. Sparking up, he inhaled gratefully, taking the smoke deep into his lungs, savoring the tightness across his chest.

A roar of thunder broke above him, followed by lightning that floodlit the grounds.

A figure in a raincoat hurried across the gravel, coming in his direction, head bowed against the rain. Rushing into the protection of the gazebo, they shook off the excess from their waterproof.

"The things we do for our addictions," Joe joked.

The figure removed their hood, and he realized it was Terry's assistant, Muriel. He almost didn't recognize her. There was something strange about her face, then he noticed she wasn't wearing her glasses.

"I didn't know you smoked," he said, offering his packet.

Muriel took her hand out of the raincoat.

The last time Joe had seen a gun, he had fired it into Sonny Rock's head.

Now he looked down the barrel of another as Muriel pointed it in his face.

Chapter Sixteen

Standing at the side of the stage, shielded from the audience, Daniel took a long, slow swallow of whiskey, savoring the heat as it ran down his throat. He'd paced his drinks, and this was only his second after the tipple he had shared with Max earlier. Even without the alcohol, he was buzzing. What a night it had been so far.

Max was out front, getting the crowd warmed up with the kind of casual banter that came so naturally to her. They didn't need much encouragement. Terry and Max had gotten them on side from the start of the night. Elijah's food, the wine, and the charity auction had stoked them to a fever pitch. The air was electric.

A nervous strain pulled in Daniel's stomach. He ignored it. The tension was good. He wasn't worried about the show. There was too much goodwill in the room. Nothing could go wrong.

Terry hadn't returned for the meal or the late show. It was just as well. It would do him more good to rest than face another audience. Bed was the best place for him.

Daniel would check on him after the show. If he wasn't asleep, he might like to come to the green room for a nightcap with the rest of the team.

Now it looked as if Joe had disappeared too. From behind the screen he could see his new boyfriend, Callum, sitting on his own. Daniel hadn't met the boy yet, but from the little he'd seen of him, they didn't look like a vision of love together. Had the attraction worn off already?

Too late to worry about them now.

Max announced him and the crowd went nuts. Daniel strode onto the stage as his music struck up, launching straight into a medley of songs from *Jersey Boys*. He planned to play it safe. Lots of big, punchy numbers that the audience would know. This was not the time to spring one of his fresh, new songs on them. No one would appreciate that.

The ten-piece mini-orchestra were a delight to sing with. He didn't know who enjoyed the show more, the spectators or him, as he ran from one song to the next. Half an hour flew by in a heartbeat and it seemed like no time at all until he was singing the final song in the set.

The audience wouldn't leave it at that. They almost deafened him with their cries. "More. More."

They stamped their feet and thumped the table tops.

"All right, all right." He laughed. "You win. I've got one more."

He sang *All Over the World*, the debut single from Overload, a song he had reclaimed and made his own. Now he sang it as an act of defiance. Against Oliver and the hate that had festered in him, a hate that had spread and claimed the lives of two of his former bandmates.

He dedicated the song to the friends he had lost, and the audience loved it.

He was a survivor—their survivor—and they appreciated everything he gave them.

"Oh, God," Daniel said as he left the stage for the final time. "That was intense."

Max waited at the side, taking him in a warm, celebratory hug. "You were amazing." She hurried back out to close the show and introduce Ben for the late-night party.

"She's right. You were incredible." Elijah was right there, still wearing his chef's outfit. He'd taken off the hat and his dark hair was in a state of sexy dishevelment. He took Daniel in his arms, holding him tight, and laid his chin on his shoulder. "I'm so proud of you. You smashed that." He smelled of the kitchen. Meaty and a little spicy.

"We smashed it," Daniel corrected. "The dinner was out of this world. I don't know how you pulled it all off. Things must have been crazy back there."

"Not so bad. To be honest, I don't remember much, it went so fast. The food got cooked and people ate it. Right now, that's all I care about."

"I'm proud of you," Daniel said, in no hurry to break the embrace, or the moment. It was just the two of them. Daniel and Elijah, cut off from the world. No noise, no stress, no people to distract them. If it could only stay like this.

"Come on," Elijah said at last, lifting his head from Daniel's shoulder and breaking the spell. "I've got something for you."

"Unless it's a warm bed and your hot body, I'm not interested."

He gave Daniel's butt a playful slap. "You'll have to wait a little longer for that."

Elijah took Daniel to the kitchen where the catering staff were gathered around a central island celebrating. They were tired, but in jubilant spirits. They had wine and beer and a huge plate of leftover food. They clapped as Daniel entered.

"Don't applaud me," he said, bringing his hands together. "You guys did the hard work tonight. You were fantastic."

"It was a team effort," Elijah said. "I think we all did great." On the counter stood a bottle of champagne in an ice bucket. "I've been saving this for us," he told Daniel, as he filled two glasses.

Daniel took one gratefully. "I'm always parched when I come off stage."

"It looks like we did it," Elijah said, moving closer, leaning against him. "We got through everything we were supposed to, without disaster. That deserves a good drink."

Daniel put a hand on his chest. "Don't tempt fate saying things like that. The night isn't over."

"No, but we're all done. There's nothing left to screw up. So, let's relax and enjoy what's left of the party."

"I'm surprised you have the energy."

"Oh, I've got lots of surprises for you in that department."

"That sounds like a promise."

"You're always on a promise from me."

"Why don't we call it a night?" Daniel suggested. "If there's nothing else for us, why don't we slip away? No one will notice. Let's take the bottle to our room." He leaned in for a kiss, touching his lips to Elijah's.

The intimacy was broken by the clatter of high heels on the tiled floor.

"Guys, guys."

It was April. She had changed since Daniel saw her last. The long evening gown she'd started the night in had been traded for a glitzy black cocktail dress, cut high on her thighs. The heels looked like six-inches plus.

"Isn't this fabulous?" April gushed. "The take so far has exceeded everyone's expectations. The auction. Oh wow. You charmed the money right out of their wallets. They were falling over themselves to give more. We must do this again. Exactly the same, Elijah's food, you and Max on the stage."

"Hang on," Elijah said, laughing. "Can we have a few hours to recover from this one first?"

"I could sell this night a hundred times over," April said, undeterred, her eyes flashing. "But next time, we need a bigger venue. This place is far too small. We'll have more tables and higher ticket prices. Just imagine how much money we'll make."

"No," Daniel said. "If there is a next time — and I'm not saying there will be — it has to be affordable."

"These people can afford it. Trust me. They want to give us their cash. You saw them. It would be a crime not to take advantage. It's for charity."

"Taking advantage doesn't sound very charitable."

April laughed. "You boys. I've a lot to teach you. But don't hang around. Elijah, you need to change."

He stared at her, puzzled. "Change for what?"

"The party."

"Oh, we were going to pass on the party. We're pretty tired."

"No," she asserted. "I need you there. Everyone does. I'm going to announce the grand total at one o'clock and I want everyone on stage for that. You can hardly step up in your greasy apron. So, change."

With a tight smile, she rotated on one of her lofty heels and marched out.

"So much for the early night." Elijah drained his glass and poured another before refreshing Daniel's.

"She's right." Daniel sighed. "We can't blow the party after all this. And I would like to know how much cash we've made."

"Then I'd better change out of my greasy apron. Into what, I don't know. I didn't bring a suit, or even a jacket. I didn't think I'd need one."

"Pants and a clean shirt will do it. Go to the room and do it now. I'd like to check in on Terry. See if he wants to come down for the finale."

They took their drinks and headed together for the stairs.

"How is he?" Elijah asked.

"He looked pretty knackered after his show and went to lie down. He said he'd come for dessert, but I haven't seen him yet. I won't push him. If he wants to stay in bed, that's the best place for him. Muriel didn't come back either. She must be watching over him."

"We've got extra desserts in the kitchen. If they want to eat in their room, tell Muriel to ring down, Magda will send up a tray."

They parted on the first floor. Terry's room was on this landing, while their own was up on the top floor.

"Have I got time for a quick shower?" Elijah asked, sniffing his armpit. "I'm a little ripe."

"If you make it quick." Daniel leaned over for a parting kiss. "See you downstairs in twenty minutes."

"If not sooner."

Daniel headed down the hall. His footsteps were muffled on the deep, red-patterned carpet. The sense of achievement was massive. They'd done it. Delivered the gala they'd promised and raised a fortune for Supporting Victims. He couldn't imagine what the final total would be, but if April was right, it was going to be huge. And if it raised the profile of the charity, even better. It would bring even more cash and help future victims of crime.

Another victory over people like Oliver and Sonny Rock.

The upper hallways of the hotel were empty. Everyone was downstairs, enjoying the party. He picked up the distant beat from the dance floor as he wandered deeper into the maze of corridors. This place was huge. He'd explored next to nothing apart from their bedroom, the function rooms and kitchen. He made a pledge to himself to check out more of the hall before they left tomorrow. It would be a waste not to. They might never come back. Elijah was so not enamored by the place, it seemed unlikely they ever would.

Following the signs, he arrived at Terry's room and knocked gently. No answer. After a few moments, he knocked again.

Still nothing.

Daniel leaned against the door, listening. Silence. No voices, no television.

Maybe Terry and Muriel were asleep.

A peculiar sensation prickled at the back of his neck. The hairs stood on edge and something tightened in his guts. A low-level sense of unease. Maybe nothing.

Maybe something.

Experience warned him not to ignore such an alarm.

He banged on the door. Louder this time.

When there was still no answer, he tried the handle. It didn't move.

"Terry," he called. "Muriel."

The ominous feeling deepened. His heart beat faster. A million ideas raced through his mind. He hadn't seen either of them in hours. Joe had been absent for a while too. And Keeley had failed to arrive after her trip to Blackpool. *Shit*. He'd been so focused on the gala he'd been blind to the bigger picture.

He reached in his jacket for his phone. It had been set to silent all evening.

He had several missed calls and one text message.

With trembling figures, he opened the text. It came from an unknown number with a multimedia attachment. A photograph. His breath came shorter as he waited for the image to load.

This was it. The moment he'd been dreading had finally arrived. The long game had reached its end.

At first, he couldn't make out what he was looking at, the image was dark and out of focus, but a chilling realization soon came over him.

It was Terry and Joe. Gagged and restrained, their lips were stretched wide around the rags in their mouths, teeth displayed. Joe's familiar eyes were wide and terrified. Terry's were closed. Was he conscious? Was he even alive?

As Daniel stared at the photo, the phone rang. The same unknown number.

"Come alone," a familiar voice said. "If you want them to live."

Chapter Seventeen

The thunder had moved over, but the rain continued at a torrential volume. Cold, every item of clothing soaked and heavy, Daniel walked along the coastal trail, oblivious to the elements. He moved forward on autopilot, until the path from the cliff descended to the beach, using the flashlight function on his phone to stay on track. The beach was dark, crooked with deeper shadows. To his right—in the pitch black—the sea pounded the shore.

Then, ahead, he saw the soft light of the cottage.

He walked purposefully toward it.

So, it had come to this. Tonight, his personal hell would end on this bleak, desolate stretch of coastline. He could never have predicted it. When he had stepped onboard *The Atlantic Anthem* in Lisbon almost two years ago, he couldn't have foreseen a single moment of it. Oliver Gill's hatred had left a long, destructive shadow, poisoning everything it touched.

With his head down, Daniel walked into the force of the wind and driving rain, focused on nothing but the cottage.

Muriel Durrell. Terry's lifelong friend and personal assistant. Of all the people he'd suspected, she was never one. Too old to be Oliver's mother. They'd focused their attention on younger women, believing the girl who abandoned her baby on a doorstep could only have been a child herself. Victim of an unwanted teenage pregnancy. She would be in her mid to late forties now. No older. He didn't consider Oliver might have been the unwanted child of an older woman.

We couldn't have been more wrong.

Every step toward the cottage was an effort. His feet sank into the sodden sand. As the waves rushed over his toes, he realized how high the tide must be. Undeterred, he pushed onward.

Daniel had left the hotel as soon as he received her call, without speaking to anyone.

'Come alone. If you want them to live.'

He didn't doubt what she said. Muriel had blood on her hands. Two more lives would make no difference to her.

He was walking into her web alone, unprotected. He didn't care. Not anymore. This had to end, and he was ready for her.

He reached the gate of the cottage. The front door opened as he walked up the path.

She stood in the frame, pointing a gun at him. Daniel did not flinch.

Muriel was quite transformed. The horn-rimmed glasses had gone, and so had the tweedy suits. Dressed in black trousers and a sweater, she stood taller and straighter. Her gray hair was swept off her face and tucked behind her ear.

So, he thought, *she's an actress too.* An accomplished one at that. Muriel Durrell was nothing but a character.

"Where are they?" he asked, rain pouring over him.

"They're here." She tipped her head into the room behind her.

"Are they alive?"

"For now."

"Let them go."

Her face was thunderous. "I have the gun and I give the orders. Get inside, slowly."

She stepped back into the hall, keeping the gun leveled at him, giving him room to pass.

With his hands raised, he stepped inside. Muriel gestured to the right. Daniel entered a small living room. The ceiling was low with exposed wooden beams. He cast his eyes around the sparse furnishings, searching for Joe and Terry. He saw them, tied together in the corner of the room, and hurried toward them.

"No," Muriel snapped. "Stay where you are, or the boy gets the first bullet."

Terry was out of it. Asleep? Unconscious? Dead? Daniel couldn't make out. His wig had fallen, revealing the fragile, bald head beneath. There was a gray, waxy pallor to his skin. His chin lay slumped against his bony chest. Joe was awake, looking at Daniel with wide, terrified eyes.

"Are you all right?" Daniel asked him.

Joe nodded, tears running in parallel down his face.

"That's enough," Muriel said, slamming the front door. She came into the room, gun raised. "Take off your jacket, slowly, and throw it behind the sofa."

Daniel shrugged off the soaking jacket. In the inside pocket was a can of mace, his only defense. Some use it would be against a firearm. Stupidly, he had left the more effective Tasers in the bedroom, figuring, as he wasn't leaving the hotel tonight, he wouldn't need them. Idiot.

"Now turn out your trouser pockets," she said.

He did what she asked. They were empty.

She nodded, satisfied, and gestured for him to move against the wall.

"I never thought it would be you," Daniel said coldly.

"Then you're an idiot. I was under your nose the entire time, and no one noticed. Blind and stupid."

"I can see it now," he said, meeting her challenging stare. "It's in your eyes. Just there. Obvious really. Just like Oliver — stark raving lunacy."

"Taunt me all you want. If you think I'm going to snap over a few insults, you're wrong. I didn't get this far by being a hotheaded reactionary."

"No, hiring Sonny Rock to do your dirty work was a sign of pure genius. You must have been thrilled with the quality of his work. Way to go, Muriel. You're such a winner."

"Sonny taught me a valuable lesson. If you want something done, do it yourself. So here I am, and there you are, about to pay the price for what you did."

He laughed, mocking her. "For what I did? Oliver, your son, he jumped off that ship all by himself. Right after he murdered one person and poisoned another. Nobody pushed him. Nobody forced him. He climbed the rail and jumped."

"Daniel, you pushed him all right. Maybe not physically, but you drove him to it. Mentally, you pushed him over the edge. You are the reason he's dead."

She believed that — it was clear in her eyes. The crazy bitch thought it was true. Daniel wasn't lying when he told her she reminded him of Oliver. They had the same hell-bent expression. "Oliver was mentally unstable long before I met him on the ship. Don't take it from me, there are dozens of statements from people who knew him before, and staff who worked with him on the *Anthem*. Oliver was a deeply unhappy man. Maybe you should look closer to home to lay the blame for that. Being dumped on a doorstep, unwanted as a baby, can't have done his self-esteem much good."

Muriel shook her head, undaunted. "That could all have been resolved if it wasn't for you. I'd already traced my baby. I knew where he was. I was ready to reach out to him. And now I can't. I never will."

"Boo-fucking-hoo," he sneered. "I know four kids who don't have fathers because of you. Parents who lost a daughter because of your fucked-up son. If you think your grief comes close to that, you're as crazy as I know you are."

"You know nothing and you never have. You're so caught up in your career, you have no time for anyone else. The people you hurt along the way, fighting to get what you wanted, they're just collateral damage to you. Like my son. You stomped all over him to get the Overload gig."

Daniel groaned. "Overload. Fuck, I wish I'd never heard of that group. If I'd known the misery it would bring, I'd have stayed well away. But Oliver was gone by the time I arrived. I attended the audition to replace him after they got rid of him. They couldn't work with him, his behavior was difficult and demanding. It was the manager, Sam, who let him go."

"Lies," she said, calm and without emotion. "Nothing but a whitewash. A cover-up." She moved across the room, keeping the gun fixed on Daniel the whole time. "The truth will come out someday. I'll make certain of that. Because nothing you have said carries any weight. Just like that miserable old bastard." She nodded toward Terry. "Can you imagine what it was like for me? Having to type the manuscript for that package of lies he calls a biography. It's bullshit, every word. I was there in the beginning. I know what it was really like."

"So, you really were friends with Terry? That part is true?"

"I knew him," she said, her lips drawing back from her teeth. "Not as well as he likes to tell it. I doubt he even remembers. The fool believes that fantasy version of his life. After Oliver's death, I was bereft. Utterly consumed with anger and sadness. I needed to do something. And there he was, Terry St. King, preening like a peacock in the spotlight, basking in his newfound attention. He was my way in. I don't think he even remembered me when I got in touch, but it didn't take much to convince him. A lot of flattery about how great he was, the good times we used to have, how underrated his talents were. A subtle suggestion that he could use a PA to manage his affairs, now he was so popular. It was pitiful really, how quick he took the bait."

It made sense. As Terry's assistant, she went with him everywhere. And since the *Anthem*, he and Terry had remained good friends, staying in touch. Muriel would know all about Daniel, his movements, where he'd be at any one time.

She moved closer to Terry and Joe, standing over them. She looked down with a murderous flash in her eyes. "That damn book of his. What a load of shit. I had to listen to it all, type the fucking words as he dictated them. All the lies he told about Oliver. The poison this rancid old crone spewed. It made me sick."

She drew back her foot and aimed a perfect kick into Terry's abdomen, stunning in its viciousness. Terry let out a grunt but did not regain consciousness.

"Stop," Daniel yelled. "No."

Her angry eyes flashed in his direction. "I could have killed this old cunt any time I wanted. A push down the stairs, a mix-up with his medication. It would have been easy to kill him without a trace of suspicion. I would have done it too, until the cancer came along, and I realized it would give him a more painful, lingering death than I could manage. I've enjoyed every agonizing minute of his suffering."

Daniel slumped against the wall. She was insane. And she could have taken them any time she wanted. Any one of them. Poisoned the wine or the water when they went to dinner the other night. It would have been easy. "You obviously went to a great deal of trouble to stage this scene. To get me to this cottage. So, come on, tell me what it's all about."

"In a little while." The anger in her face faded. "I want to tell you my story."

"Oh, God. Why should I believe a word of it? You're a murderer."

"Not yet I'm not."

"Don't delude yourself about your innocence. Sonny Rock was your instrument, just like the gun in your hand. You're a liar. A fraud. A killer."

"What I'm going to tell you is all true, I can assure you of that." She looked at her watch. "We've got a little time before they notice you're missing. Not much, but I'll keep it brief. My story won't take long. It's simple enough."

She was right. Given all that had happened to them, Elijah would not waste time in raising the alarm once he knew Daniel was missing. Would he even remember this place, to focus a search in this direction? He doubted it, but the longer he kept her talking, the more time it would give them. *Come on, Elijah, don't hang about.*

"All right," he said. "Let's hear it."

She laughed softly to herself. "Hard to believe looking at me now, but I was once a young, slim, exquisite blonde."

"You're right. That is hard to believe."

"In the late 1960s, Muriel Durrell from Blackpool moved to London to pursue a career in the big city. She changed her name to Martine Ewing and did all right for herself, for a while at least. I was gorgeous, and that opened a lot of doors. Modeling, acting, eye candy on the arms of powerful men. I had some good movie and TV roles. Carry On Films. *Hammer Horror*, I did a few episodes of *Doctor Who* and auditioned for a James Bond movie. Bit parts and set dressing mostly, but I was out there, getting my face seen by the right people. But mainly I worked in cabaret clubs and stage shows. The dolly-bird parts fizzled out in the seventies, but I kept working in the clubs, which is where I met Terry. We were never as tight as I've led him to believe, but we were on the same bills a lot of the time."

"So that's where Oliver got it from," Daniel said, taunting her. "He inherited your drive to be something big in showbusiness. Let me guess, you never made it either."

"Quite right," she said, refusing to bite. "But, unlike Oliver, I gave it up. It became too weary. Traveling around the country, appearing on bills with third-rate acts like Terry St. King. The 1970s were a lot different from how things are now. The clubs we were playing were the pits, working men's shitholes in the backend of nowhere. Getting changed in the toilets, or the beer cellar if we were lucky, painting on a smile to entertain the drunken riffraff. I remember Terry being booed off stage on more than one occasion. He didn't put that in his book. I was under no illusion. There was no glamour to the kind of showbusiness we were peddling. I wanted better than that. More to life than travelling the bowels of the North in a crappy old van. In 1978, I got married to a businessman called Bobby Boyce and retired."

"Businessman?"

Muriel laughed. "Terry's manner of whitewashing the past has rubbed off on me. Bobby was a gangster. He ran a sizeable racket in Birmingham and the West Midlands. I didn't care. I hadn't had a decent gig in over a year when I met him, hadn't had a film part in five. Bobby had a big house and nice cars. He bought me furs and jewelry. He was as ugly as sin and it did his image good to be seen with a glamourous starlet even if she was past her prime."

"Was he Oliver's father?" Daniel asked. "No, he couldn't be. You wouldn't have gotten rid of the baby if he was. So, who? You had an affair?"

"Don't get ahead of yourself. You wanted to know my story, so listen. My marriage was a disaster on a physical level. I didn't want Bobby and he sure as shit didn't want me. He was more interested in young girls and hookers. Scrubbers, the lot of them. I was the stay-at-home wife, living in luxury and wheeled out to join him when he wanted to look good at public occasions. Except, sitting at home all day with nothing to do, I put on weight. Not a huge amount but enough to show. I went from dolly bird to frumpy housewife in a few years. I was happy to let myself go, to not have to make the effort, for a while at least. Until one day I looked in the mirror and didn't recognize myself. I was thirty-five and looked much older. More like fifty.

"I joined an exercise class. Aerobics were all the rage in the eighties and the weight came off easier than I expected. I loved those classes. The buzz of a good workout was addictive, almost as addictive as the results I was getting. I couldn't wait to go to the next session, so I hired a personal trainer to help me chase that buzz. David, his name was. I can't even remember his surname, but he was very good-looking as you can imagine. Young too, barely in his twenties. I hadn't been with a man like that in years. You can guess the rest."

He nodded. "How did you keep it a secret?"

"Easily. Bobby barely looked at me, let alone came near. He just thought I was getting fat again."

"Did David know you were pregnant?"

Another cold laugh. "I told him and never saw him again. Our personal sessions were over. I didn't fool myself that he'd want me or the baby. He had a girlfriend his own age, and a pocketbook of horny housewives to service. He was a kid himself. No way could he look after a baby."

"Okay. I get that. But you weren't a kid. Why did you abandon the baby? You could have left Bobby and looked after Oliver on your own."

"Bobby was a gangster. I'm not talking about minor fiddles and book-making scams. He was the real deal. Dangerous and mean. If he'd found out about the baby, he'd have killed it. And me. David too, if he ever caught him. There was no way I could keep the baby. And I hadn't had sex with Bobby in years, so fooling him the kid was his was out of the question. I knew from the beginning the best thing to do was give the child away. Doing that legitimately was out of the question, Bobby would have found out, so I wrapped him up warm and left him in a doorway."

Her voice cracked, betraying her first trace of emotion other than hatred. She took a deep breath and ran her tongue over her teeth before continuing.

"I gave birth in an empty flat my husband owned and left him in Blackpool, my home town. I knew he'd be all right there. That someone would care for him. And I left him in a place he would be found quickly." She took another great breath, sobbing. "It's the clearest, most profound memory of my life. The look on my baby's face when I said goodbye to him. Swaddled in blankets, so innocent, he had everything ahead of him. Everything except a mother. He could never have me and I could never have him."

How long had she been talking? It seemed a while. Surely someone had noticed they were gone by now. Daniel threw a quick glance toward Terry and Joe. Joe was awake, listening, but Terry was still out of it. Still breathing? He couldn't make out. *Please, let him get through this.*

"That must have been terrible for you," he said, giving his voice a sympathetic tone he did not feel. A woman giving up her baby was a tragedy in any circumstance, but Muriel Durrell had given up her right to sympathy the moment she arranged the murders to avenge her lost son.

"Save it," she snapped, wiping her eyes on the back of her hand. "I don't need your pity. You of all people, you disgust me."

"You were right," he continued undeterred. "Oliver was adopted in Blackpool. He found a family there. You did the right thing for him."

"I followed his progress. It was easy enough in the beginning. The papers had plenty to report, but in the end, I had to let go. Bobby could never know what I'd done. If he did, he'd have found the boy and killed him, and then killed me."

He wondered how much of her account had been adapted to suit her own way of thinking. He couldn't imagine any man, no matter how ruthless, being cruel enough to murder a child. Life might not have been a dream for Muriel, but he couldn't believe Oliver was ever at risk.

"I got on with my life," she continued. "Consumed with regret, with guilt, but content that I'd done the right thing for the boy. For my boy. Around seven years ago, Bobby became ill. Terminal. The bastard was finally on his way out. It was still a risk, but I traced Oliver. I wanted to know how he was doing, what he'd made of his life. It was a shock to learn that I'd already seen him on TV. I used to watch your TV show *The One*. Like everyone else, I'd laughed at Oliver's audition, at his meltdown when he didn't get through. And how he'd turn up on all those tacky shows afterward, trying to prolong his fifteen minutes of fame, while you soared all the way to the top. I even voted for you.

"I felt sick with myself. This boy, this figure of public ridicule, was my son, my baby, and I didn't even recognize him. I didn't try to make contact. The time still wasn't right, not while Bobby was alive, but I came to love him. I followed him on the internet. I watched his videos and looked at his photos, knowing one day, soon, we'd be reunited."

She paused. Her eyes, the gun, still trained on Daniel, but her focus was elsewhere, somewhere inward. She was a deeply disturbed woman. Was there any way to reason with her? Did she possess any reason?

"Those TV shows edited Oliver in a bad light," Daniel lied. "He wasn't like that in real life." No, he was worse. The swearing, the racism, sexism, none of it had been fit for broadcast on a family TV show. Oliver was a spiteful, poisonous creature. Daniel didn't believe that came from being abandoned as a baby. His stepsister Rachel showed what a secure, loving environment he'd been raised in. In all likelihood more normal than anything Muriel could have given him. Oliver would have turned out the same under Muriel's care, possibly worse.

"I'll never know. When Bobby died, when I finally had the opportunity to reach out to my son, it was too late. You had killed him."

"I did not kill Oliver. He tried to kill me."

"You and him." She pointed at Terry. "You were there together when he died. I don't believe the old man had the strength to throw Oliver overboard, but you did."

"I'd been stabbed. Oliver jumped. It didn't happen any other way. He jumped."

"So you say."

There was no reasoning with her. The best he could do now was stall for time. Keep her talking in the hope someone would find them.

"What about Sonny? Was he just a heavy who worked for your husband?"

"He was exactly that. An enforcer, a bit of muscle. He was also a psychopath with a mother-complex. He was just seventeen when he came to work for Bobby and had an eye for me even then. I was sixty-two when my husband died. You might not believe it, looking at me now in my Muriel-drag, but I still had it. The old showgirl was in there, a little curvier than before, but I could turn on the charm in a heartbeat. Sonny lapped it up. This psycho who enjoyed hurting people was a pussycat in my arms. When it was time to take revenge on you all, Sonny was exactly the man for the job."

"He fucked it up."

She nodded. "Yes. It was his idea to go after Overload. To kill the other members of the group. I didn't care about them. They weren't on the ship the night Oliver died. I was only interested in you, but Sonny thought it would be neat to kill the others too. He wanted to hurt more people. I should have stopped him."

"But you didn't. You let him kill two men, two fathers."

She shrugged. "I learnt my lesson. I would have to do it myself. I was already in with Terry. Part of me must have suspected that Sonny would fail, so I'd already set Plan B in motion. Getting in touch with the old fool, flattering him, gaining his trust, making myself indispensable. It was a nightmare. Cozying up to him every minute of the day. Still, it paid off in the end. We're here now aren't we." She smiled.

"You stupid, lunatic bitch," he sneered. "All of this — people dead, lives ruined — all because of you. A bored housewife who got herself knocked up and was too cowardly to face the consequences."

"Shut up."

"No. Every step of the way, when you had a decision to make, you made the wrong choice. You ruined everything. For you and your son."

"Quiet," she screamed.

"Oliver was exactly like you. You should be proud, Muriel. He was a grade A fuck-up too. And rotten to the core, just like his mother."

"Enough," she said, standing straight, both hands on the gun. "I've done you a favor. You'll go to your grave knowing the answers. And that's as far as my generosity extends. This is over."

He glared at her defiantly. "Shoot me. C'mon, do it so I don't have to listen to any more of your bullshit."

Muriel slowly shook her head, a vindictive grin etched across his face. "Shoot you? I don't think so. That would be too easy. I'll shoot this pair if you don't do what I say, but a bullet is too quick for you. I have something more rewarding in mind."

"Do what you want, it won't bring Oliver back."

"No, but it'll give me some peace. My son died at sea. Cold and alone, in the fiercest of waters. Someone up there is on my side tonight, sending this storm. You're going the same way, Daniel. You're going to die out there, in that sea, where no one will hear you. No one can save you."

Chapter Eighteen

Coming downstairs, showered and refreshed, Elijah found himself swept up in a sea of congratulations. Everyone wanted to commend him on the food, pat his back, shake his hand, lean in for kisses.

"You must write down your recipes for a book."

"Where do you get your supplies?"

"Do you cater private parties?"

April, hovering at the entrance of the function room, came to his rescue, taking him aside.

"This is the best I could manage," he said, showing her the black trousers and white shirt he'd changed into, with a blazer borrowed from Daniel's wardrobe.

"You look very handsome," April said, straightening his shirt collar, "but now I've lost Daniel. Have you seen him?"

"Check the dance floor," he said. From inside the hall, the unmistakable sound of Max LaFranchi's club hit *Roses and Rainbows* issued. A sure-fire floor filler. Daniel wouldn't miss the opportunity to dance to it.

"I'll look," she said. "Don't go away. I want to make the announcement soon and I need you all present. Tonight's total is out of this world."

"How much?"

"Wait and see," she said, clicking away on her heels.

Elijah needed a drink. A proper one. "I'll be in the green room," he called after her, and headed upstairs to the first floor.

The hospitality suite was deserted. No surprise. Everyone would be in the hall. By the sound of things, Ben had quite a party going. At the bar, Elijah helped himself to a large vodka, ice and a splash of Coke. The first mouthful hit the spot.

The shower and change of clothes had gone someway to reviving him, but he was beat. Today had been a challenge. He wanted to go to bed and sleep for a minimum of eight hours.

There was a hesitant knock at the door. Elijah turned as Callum entered, looking sheepish.

"Oh hi, have you seen Joe? I thought he might be up here."

"Lost him, have you?"

Callum came closer. "I haven't seen him in a while. He won't answer his phone. I think I might have blown it."

Elijah was about to pour Callum a vodka when he got a whiff of his breath. He reeked of booze already. He passed him a mineral water instead. "What happened?"

Callum's shoulders slumped. "I've been a dick. I kind of...got carried away. A little star-struck by Daniel. A lot star-struck. I didn't pay Joe the attention he deserved."

"When did you see him last?"

"He went for a cigarette after the meal. I haven't seen him since. I checked the smoking area, but there's no one out there."

"Maybe he went to bed early."

"I checked the room too, he's not there. I think I've been dumped."

Judging by his bratty behavior, Elijah wasn't surprised. Callum was immature, a kid. Joe had done a lot of growing up in the last year. He thought they might have been good for each other, but it was obvious they were too far apart, at different stages of their lives. Before the attack, they would have been an ideal match. Not anymore.

"Is this a free bar?" Callum put the unopened water bottle on the counter and helped himself to the vodka, pouring a quadruple measure. "Might as well make the most of it."

Elijah didn't stop him. He wouldn't see him again after tomorrow.

"Where's Daniel?" Callum asked.

"Downstairs, someplace."

Callum licked his lips, giving Elijah a long, lascivious look. "You make a good couple."

"I know."

"Hot too. I don't suppose you...play around? Do you?"

Oh, please. "We do not," he replied firmly. A drunken come-on. Could Callum make the situation any worse?

The answer was yes.

"Would you like to?" He came closer, stroking his groin. "I think you're both really hot. How about it? The two of you and me. You can do anything you want. Use me real good."

"No."

"Come in my butt. Come on my face. Anything you like."

"Jesus, Callum, no." He thrust the bottle of water back in his direction. "Drink that. You need to sober up. And grow up."

Elijah left him before he got any other stupid ideas. Poor Joe, he deserved better than this loser. A lot better. To make it worse, Elijah had encouraged them. Joe hadn't wanted to go out with Callum, not in the beginning. He'd urged him to do it. Big mistake. He'd have to make it up to him.

He got downstairs without being accosted and headed straight to the hall. The dance floor was heaving but there was no sign of Daniel. Maybe April had found him already. Skirting the edges of the room, he headed back to the foyer.

There was a commotion at the front door. Two security offices were arguing with a woman in the entrance.

"Check your fucking guest list," the woman snapped. "You'll find I'm on it."

He recognized her voice — Keeley — and changed direction.

No wonder they didn't want to let her in. Dressed in jeans and a waist-length jacket, Keeley was soaked through. Her usually immaculate blonde hair clung to her head in ratty strands.

"It's okay," Elijah said, intervening. "She's a guest."

"Elijah, thank God." She pushed straight past the disgruntled bouncers.

"What happened? I didn't think you were coming."

"I've had a nightmare getting here," she said, pushing back her hair. Out of breath, she grabbed his arm. "I'm glad to see you're okay. Where's Daniel?"

"He's inside. Why?"

Then he knew. The expression on Keeley's face confirmed it. The moment they feared most had come. It had stolen upon them while they weren't looking.

"Who is it?"

"Muriel Durrell. Terry's frumpy PA. Have you seen her?"

"No. Not for hours. What? Muriel is Oliver's mother?"

She nodded grimly. "I've been trying to warn you, but none of the fucking phones work."

Muriel? What? No, it can't be.

Keeley took his arm and led him away from the crowd of eavesdroppers.

"She's been under our noses the whole time," Keeley said. "I found an ex-con in Blackpool who served time in prison with Sonny. All the while they were banged up he said Sonny had a hard-on for some old scrubber. Twenty-odd years older than he was. The wife of his boss."

"How does that tie into Muriel?"

"Sonny was serving time for robbery. Nasty stuff. He beat the living daylights out of a poor post office manager. Sonny kept his mouth shut and served the time. He worked for Bobby Boyce, a gangster running rackets in Birmingham. Bobby was married to Martine Ewing, a two-bit actress and showgirl."

"So? What does that have to do with Muriel?"

"Martine Ewing was a stage name. Her real name is Muriel Durrell."

"But Muriel? A gangster's moll and showgirl? You've got it wrong. You must have."

"It's her all right," Keeley said. "Older, heavier. Martine Ewing was a dolly bird. All makeup, hair and tits, but strip that away, and it's Muriel underneath."

He shook his head, struggling to put it together. "How is she Oliver's mother?"

"Okay, that's where I had to fill in a few details for myself, but I'm sure they'll check out. Oliver was dumped on a doorstep when he was a baby. That much we know. Muriel would have been in her mid-thirties at the time. Bobby Boyce was a womanizer. They'd been married around ten years. I'm betting Bobby didn't have much interest in his wife after all that time. So, Muriel plays away. Who can blame her? She was fucking Sonny on and off for years while her old man was still alive, so we know she's not above that kind of thing. My guess is she got pregnant by another man, kept it a secret, then ditched the baby when it was born."

Elijah's heart raced. This was crazy. He couldn't take it in. "How sure are you?"

"Ninety-nine percent. C'mon, it makes sense. Muriel started working for Terry after Oliver's death. She reverted to her maiden name so no one would know who she is. She was involved with Sonny, the man who tried to kill you, and she said nothing about it. Elijah, I'm telling you, she's it."

"Fuck." His head pounded. He needed to act fast. It might already be too late. "Hey," he shouted at the security men on the door. "Emergency. Lock down the hotel, let no one out. And call the police. Tell them Daniel Blake's life is at risk."

"Where is he?" Keeley asked.

"We need to find out." He raced to the reception desk. The receptionist, a woman in her forties, was already on her feet. "Have you seen Daniel?"

She shook her head. "Not for an hour at least."

"Do you have a pass key to all the rooms?" Keeley asked.

"Yes."

"Bring it. You have to let us into Terry St. King's room."

She did as they asked, taking them upstairs and unlocking the door.

It was empty. Both beds unslept in.

"Get on to security," Elijah told the receptionist. "Tell them to check the CCTV for Daniel and a woman in her mid-sixties. We need to search every room in this hotel until we find them."

The woman got straight onto her walkie-talkie, issuing instructions.

Elijah slammed his fist into his palm. They'd been so stupid. So blind. Why had it taken so long to uncover the truth?

The bitch. She'd played them for fools.

Daniel was in trouble. The worst kind.

The feeling of hopeless impotence was crushing.

Where the hell are they?

Elijah would tear this place apart to find them. And if he got his hands on Muriel Durrell, he would tear her to pieces.

Chapter Nineteen

Daniel didn't fight as Muriel tied his hands behind his back. It would have been pointless. She got the stainless-steel cuffs on him with one hand, keeping the barrel of the gun tight into the middle of his back. She would shoot. He had no doubt about it. Having listened to her story, and learned the depths of her rage, he believed her capable of anything. She displayed no trace of empathy for the people who had died so far — Anouska Frost, Luke Torrens, Christian Gates — or the families they'd left behind. Cold and brutal, Muriel had no heart. It would be pointless to appeal for kindness. She would shoot him in the back if he fought, then kill Terry and Joe out of spite.

She'd gone too far to pull back. The best he could do was stall for time and pray Elijah was on his way. A desperate hope. Elijah would know he was missing by now, but he'd never trace him to this place.

"Were you a singer?" he asked.

"What?"

"You said you were a cabaret star. Were you a singer? I wondered whether Oliver inherited that talent from you."

The question appeared to throw her. *Keep talking about Oliver. It's the one advantage you have. You know the son she didn't.*

"He was good," Daniel continued. "Better than he gave himself credit for. He rubbed people up the wrong way, that was his problem. But never his singing. If he'd attempted to get along with everyone, he'd have gone far."

"Bullshit," she said. "He was going nowhere. I watched all those videos of him performing. He was a third-rate talent. That's what he inherited from me. His career was no different from mine. I had to fight for every damn slot I got on the cabaret circuit. Kissing arses and sucking maggoty cocks to stay on the bottom end of the bill. Oliver was no different. But he could have been. He could have learned from me and my mistakes."

"You're wrong about him. He was a decent singer. A real talent."

Muriel jabbed the gun into his back. "Keep talking and I'll blow your spine out right here. I know what you're doing and stalling for time won't get you anywhere. Nobody knows where you are. No one is coming to rescue you. Like no one rescued my son. Now move."

She forced him at gunpoint to the front door and told him to open it.

The rain had stopped but strong winds still gusted across the beach. In the darkness, the surf boomed against the shore. Behind him, Muriel clicked on a torchlight, illuminating the path in front of him.

"Walk," she said. "Turn left at the gate and head down the beach. Don't try anything stupid or Elijah will have to pick bits of your skull out of the sand."

A bitter North Sea wind tore through his wet clothes. When his teeth chattered, Daniel couldn't be sure if it was from the cold or through fear. He stumbled on the uneven sand, almost going down. Muriel flashed her torch across the beach ahead.

"Keep moving," she shouted above the thunderous noise.

What was the crazy bitch going to do? Walk him into the sea?

With his hands cuffed behind his back, what chance would he stand? Slight. Even without the restraints, he wouldn't last long in seas as rough as this.

"You don't have to do this," he shouted back at her. "It's not too late to stop. You haven't killed anyone yet. If you stop now, the worst you could be charged with is being an accessory to the murders of Sonny Rock."

"No, the worst that could happen is that I don't avenge my son. You're going to die, Daniel. That's the only thing that matters to me. That you die."

* * * *

At the party, the guests knew something was up. A large crowd had gathered in the foyer by the time Elijah and Keeley came downstairs. They weren't stupid. As security staff put the hotel on lockdown, they were quick to jump to conclusions. Daniel Blake, Elijah Mann and a security threat. Those things were no coincidence. Lightning hadn't just struck twice, it had hit a third time.

With a sickening instinct, Elijah realized that these people were excited at the prospect. Being caught up in the drama. They had their phones out, eager for the spectacle. Then, as they spotted him on the stairway, those phones were turned in his direction, all cameras trained on him.

"Ignore them," Keeley said, grabbing his arm, hurrying him away from the crowd. "Ghoulish fuckers."

Now he didn't care. They could film what they wanted as long as he found Daniel. As long as he was safe.

He would rip the place apart until he found them. And when he did, he would tear Muriel Durrell into a million fucking pieces.

A guard stood blocking the kitchen door. Elijah rushed over, pointing at his radio. "Have you heard anything?"

He shook his head. "They are still checking the CCTV, sir. Please keep calm until we know more."

Keep calm. Is he serious? Oh, God, where are they?

Why had he let Daniel wander off on his own? He'd learned nothing from the *Anthem*, or from Blackpool. He should have stuck with him, insisted he come upstairs while he changed. On his own, Daniel was in greater danger. Muriel had been waiting for that, counting on it. Anticipating the moment he'd leave Daniel alone before she struck.

Elijah paced the kitchen floor. He'd never felt so helpless, so impotent, so fucking useless.

"How long has she been planning this?" he asked.

Keeley had taken a cigarette from her purse and clicked angrily at a lighter to get it going. "She must have got to work on Sonny soon after Oliver's death.

When he fucked things up last year, she must have been biding her time, waiting for the right moment."

"For what? What's her plan? Terry is missing. According to his boyfriend, so is Joe. Why not me? Why take them and not me?"

"I don't know. My best guess is because she's fucking nuts. It'll make some kind of sense in that messed-up brain of hers."

The security guard suddenly snapped to attention, pressing his finger to his earpiece, listening.

"What is it?" Elijah said, hurrying back to him. They had something. *They must have something. Come on, please.*

The guard raised his other hand to silence him, stone-faced as he listened to the feed in his ear. Elijah went crazy with the wait. At last, the man turned back to him. "We've got CCTV footage of Mr. Blake leaving the hotel around eleven forty, by one of the back entrances, toward the rose garden."

"Alone? Or with Muriel?"

"He was alone. The last sighting shows him leaving the grounds in the direction of the sea. The cameras stop at the edge of the garden. Do you have any idea where he might be heading?"

The sea. The mad bitch wanted to bring this full circle. Elijah saw it clearly. Oliver died at sea so that's where she was taking Daniel. What was out there beyond the gardens? Where could they be heading? *Think. For Christ's sake, think.*

The coastal path that leads to the beach. There's nothing else there except...

"The cottage," he shouted. "There's a cottage down by the water. That has to be it."

He barged past the guard to get to the back door. He had to get down there before it was too late.

Hold on, Daniel, I'm coming for you.

* * * *

They had reached the end of the beach. Muriel's torch illuminated a jagged bluff of rocks, stretching out into the furious sea.

"Keep going," she told him.

"We've nowhere else to go."

"On to the rocks," she commanded. "Out there."

Daniel turned to look at her. Her expression was triumphant. Gloating. Two years in the planning, she was about to achieve her goal.

"This won't bring him back," Daniel said.

"Of course it won't. You made sure of that. But it will bring me closure. Now, get moving."

"You're mad."

"I am," she said, her voice calm. "And if you make me shoot you here, I promise you it'll be harder for the rest of them. I'll throw the boy into the sea, and that ridiculous old man. Then there's Elijah, I won't kill him. Not straight away. The pain of losing you will be punishment enough to begin with. But it won't end there. I'm a patient woman, you know that already. I'll bide my time before I take care of him. And when I do, it won't be painless."

He stared at her incredulously. "And if I do what you want?"

"A bullet each for Terry and the boy. It'll be quick and painless. And I'll leave Elijah to his grief."

Unsteadily, Daniel climbed the rock. He'd given up hope for himself, Muriel had won, but it might not be too late for the others. There was a chance, a slim chance, that security would find the cottage before she returned.

The going was tough. With his hands behind his back, it was impossible to keep balance on the wet, rutted outcrop. The wind strengthened as he climbed higher. His foot slipped into a fissure. His ankle twisted, a jarring pain that made him cry out loud. He fell to his knees, and another pain tore through him as he hit the hard, uneven surface.

Muriel kicked him in the back. "Get up. If I have to shoot you here my promise still stands. A slow painful end for Terry, Joe and Elijah. I might finish off the rest of Overload, just for completion. And that stupid bitch Max for good measure. Why not? I've always hated the insipid cunt. Now, move."

Daniel struggled to his feet, the pain in his ankle excruciating. He stumbled on.

The outcrop narrowed as it advanced into the sea. Up ahead, huge waves crashed over its surface.

"That's far enough," Muriel said, seemingly satisfied.

The sea was a rolling, seething nightmare, smashing against the rocks on either side of him. Daniel was unsteady on his feet, and the wind tore at him, buffering, threatening to tip him over. His teeth chattered. His entire frame trembled.

This is it. Facing the end.

"Jump," Muriel commanded.

"I...can't." His entire body had stiffened, petrified. He stared, wide-eyed, at the furious breakers. Salt water stung his eyes.

"Do it," she snapped.

He didn't answer. He couldn't. He had frozen.

A sudden shove. Muriel's full weight in the center of his back. Time expanded as he went over, making him aware of every prolonged second. Falling. Falling. The thunder of the waves, coming closer, louder.

The shock, the cold, as he fell headfirst into the cruel sea.

Nothing but blackness above and below him.

Instinct drew him toward the surface. With his hands fastened behind his back, Daniel kicked upward, but before he could break water and gasp for breath, the sea tore him under and smashed him against the rocks.

* * * *

Elijah, followed by Keeley, raced along the coastal path, using the flashlights on their phones to illuminate the way. They'd left the hotel without waiting for the security team to get their shit together. There was no time to wait. As the trail descended to the beach, he saw the lights of the cottage ahead.

His intuition had been right. They were here.

What the hell had Daniel been thinking? Coming alone.

Elijah ran faster. He didn't know what he was racing toward, all he cared about was finding Daniel.

The front door of the cottage was open. He slowed as he reached the front path, listening, hearing nothing. He went inside.

Joe, bundled in the corner, shouted through the tape that covered his mouth, bouncing up and down for attention.

Elijah hurried to him, taking in the scene. Terry was next to him, tied and gagged just the same. The old guy might already be dead. No sign of Daniel or Muriel. Carefully, Elijah peeled the tape from Joe's mouth.

Keeley burst into the room behind him. She didn't waste time, going straight for Terry, feeling for a pulse. "He's alive," she gasped. "Just."

"Where are they?" Elijah asked, when he'd taken the tape from Joe. "Where's Daniel?"

"She's taken him," Joe blurted. "Muriel. She's insane. She's...she's Oliver's mother."

"We know that. Where did she take him?"

"She's gonna throw him in the sea. They went down the beach. That way." He jerked his head in the direction.

"Go after them," Keeley shouted. "I'll untie these two."

Elijah was already on his feet and moving out the door. At the cottage gate, he turned left and ran, adrenaline giving him a speed he'd never known.

Fear threatened to consume him, but he held it back. All that mattered was reaching Daniel before it was too late.

* * * *

The water was merciless. Throwing him back and forth like a child's toy in a washing machine. It sucked him into the rocks, bashing him against the rough edges, before pushing him away. Daniel kicked for the surface. Barely catching a breath before being dragged under again. With his hands tied behind his back, it was impossible to stay afloat.

And it was cold. Colder than anything he'd ever known.

Breaking the surface again, he caught sight of Muriel on the outcrop, watching him, enjoying her victory.

The effort was too much. His energy depleted fast.

He fought for life, knowing it was useless.

When the water took him down again, he knew it was for the last time.

* * * *

Elijah reached the outcrop. His lungs seared with the effort.

He saw Muriel up ahead. She was alone.

No. He was already too late.

She had her flashlight trained on the water, watching intently. He followed her line of sight.

Daniel. His head broke water for a precious second before he went under again.

That brief glimpse of hope was all Elijah needed. He flew across the rocks, racing straight past Muriel, and threw himself headfirst into the sea. He went down, striking out in the direction he had last seen Daniel, with no care for the danger he was in. Singularly focused. Reach Daniel. Nothing else mattered.

The sea fought back. Pushing him, dragging him off course. He came up for air and caught a fleeting glimpse of Daniel ahead. Elijah powered toward him.

* * * *

Muriel saw Elijah the moment before he hit the water. *What the fuck!* Where had he come from?

Looking back down the beach, she saw he was alone. There was no one else coming. She turned her light on the sea, searching.

Let him try to save his lover. They would both die, claimed by the sea that had taken her son. Poetic justice.

She explored the white peaks with her light. Where had they gone? She'd waited too long for this moment. She wouldn't miss it.

Elijah's head broke the water, about twenty feet from where she stood. He was not alone. Head back in the water, he hoisted Daniel above the surface, pushing away from the rocks.

No. No, goddammit.

She wouldn't let them live. Not after everything.

Muriel raised her gun and pointed at their heads as they rose and fell in the surf. She fired.

* * * *

The bullet flew past Elijah's head, missing by inches. The mad bitch knew how to shoot.

Holding Daniel under the arms, keeping him afloat, he shouted, "We need to get away from her. Can you kick?"

"Yes," he answered, already thrusting with his legs.

Gripping tighter—he would never let Daniel go again—Elijah kicked too. They had to get out of range. It was far from easy, battling the sea in clothes that grew heavier by the moment. The cold penetrated to the bone.

Muriel's second shot fell a yard short. Still dangerously close.

She wouldn't have them. He was determined of that. Daniel was his. He would protect him to the end. And if the end was now, they would die together, at the mercy of the sea, not a mad woman with a gun.

The shore was to their left. If they could get away from the turbulent pull of the rocks, they stood a chance.

"Keep pushing," he encouraged Daniel. "We're going to make it."

But he knew they wouldn't. Daniel grew heavier with every thrust. He'd been in the water too long. He was weakening. Unlike the sea, which seemed stronger with every wave.

Elijah wouldn't give in. Cold gripped him, numbing every part of his body. There were no stars. No moon.

He would not give up.

"I've got you," he cried. "I've got you."

Suddenly there was hope. His legs, treading water, touched the bottom. Sand, not rock. Then he heard the distant sound of sirens, getting louder. Raising his head from the water, he saw flashing lights racing in the direction of the cottage.

Finding steadier ground, he put both feet down, dragging Daniel toward the shore. The water came up to their chests.

And they were not alone. There were hands on him, hauling them into shallower water.

Keeley and Joe.

With their help, he made it to the safety of the beach.

Daniel was frozen in his arms. Cold and unresponsive. "Get blankets," he shouted. "And an ambulance, fast."

He lay down on top of him, trying to offer the heat of his own body. But he had none. Hypothermia had taken hold of them both.

* * * *

Muriel saw the police and the ambulance. Worst of all, she saw Daniel and Elijah make it out of the water. Then her vision deteriorated in a blur of tears. She raised the gun and fired wildly. Again and again, until the cartridge was empty.

With a cry of rage, she threw the useless weapon into the sea.

There were voices. Security staff from the hotel, clambering over the rocks toward her.

It was over. *Yes.*

Finished. *No.*

She might be defeated but she would not go on their terms. Muriel Durrell, mother of Oliver Gill, would not end her days in prison.

She would join the baby she had never known in the quiet depths of the sea.

As the security men clambered toward her, Muriel walked calmly to the edge of the outcrop, and without looking back, she stepped into the deep and did not resurface.

Epilogue

Nine months later

The Atlantic Anthem cruised south on the ocean she took her name from, somewhere east of Madeira, en route to the Canary Islands. Wind and sea conditions were good, and the forecast predicted more of the same. It was set to be a perfect voyage.

On deck sixteen, on the lawn of a sun terrace laid with real grass, a small party of guests gathered. The terrace had been set with rows of chairs and decorated with beautiful displays of flowers. As the guests mingled, waiters moved among them with trays of champagne and canapés. A string quartet played classical music in the corner.

Keeley Rank wore a long white dress with a pattern of red roses. She had tucked a flower behind her ear to set off the look. She'd been the center of attention since she'd come onboard. As well she might be. *Anthem of Hate*, her true-life account of the Daniel Blake saga, had been a runaway success. She'd always known it would be. The book had spent six weeks at the top of the nonfiction bestseller chart and showed no sign of being usurped. Why should it? The book had everything — sex, murder, revenge, drugs, bastard children and long-held secrets, and amid that darkness, there was love. Daniel and Elijah's love for each other could not be broken.

That was what made her book a winner.

Other writers had been quick to cash in and rush-release their version of the story before her, but only Keeley had the full facts. She'd written the book everyone wanted to read.

The body of Muriel Durrell had been recovered from the sea three days after she had gone missing. Bloated and waterlogged, she'd become tangled in the nets of some poor fisherman. A gruesome end, but Keeley had no sympathy for the woman. She'd married a gangster for his money and the lifestyle it could provide. When an unplanned pregnancy had threatened that existence, she'd gotten rid of the baby. And thirty years later, consumed by bitterness and regret, she had taken the frustration of her failure out on innocent people. No one shed a tear for Muriel Durrell. She'd gotten what she deserved. If she had died sooner, more people might be alive now. Though Keeley wouldn't be the author of the book of the moment.

Yes, she told herself, sipping the delicious champagne, *it all worked out in the end. Well done.*

It was her gift. To uncover truths and tell the stories no one else could.

Long may it continue.

* * * *

"God, that woman doesn't half love herself."

Max LaFranchi's eyes were focused on Keeley, on the other side of the terrace.

"Ignore her," Ben said. "She's not hurting you."

"*Yet*," Max said. "She's not hurting me *yet*."

Ben put an arm around his wife's waist and lead her to the railing. "Look out there," he said, spreading his hand across the vast expanse of ocean. Nothing but blue sea and sky in every direction, not a speck of land in sight. "Don't waste time dwelling on that shit. Not when we've got all this."

She leaned into his tall frame, her head barely reaching the height of his armpit. What a guy. While she fixated on that odious woman, Keeley, Ben saw the beauty all around them. She was lucky to have found him.

They had been married for almost a year now and the romance showed no sign of waning. They were inseparable. At home and at work. Ben had produced her new album, slated for release at the end of summer. He'd also written most of the songs for her, perfectly capturing the diva persona she was known for and bringing it right up to date with a current sound that could sit side by side in the charts with the likes of Madonna and Kylie Minogue. He had also produced Daniel's new album of self-penned material, on which Max joined him for a duet. The song *Watch Out for Dangerous Men* would be the lead single when the album came out this autumn. It was sure to be a smash. Ben's production brought out the very best from both of them. She couldn't wait to perform the song live.

Ben grabbed another two glasses of champagne from a passing waiter, handing one to her.

"Are you trying to get me drunk?" she asked.

"Maybe," he said, dimples cutting his cheeks. "Would you object?"

"As long as I remember the wedding afterward."

"Oh, I think we can pace ourselves until after the ceremony." He leaned in for a kiss on the lips. She surrendered happily.

"Can you guys save it till you get back to your stateroom?"

They broke apart as Terry St. King came up behind them, with his escort for the day, Joe Elliott. Max squealed, letting go of Ben to take Terry in a warm embrace. Even better, she realized as she hugged him that Terry had put some weight on. Naturally he'd made an effort for the wedding, in a brilliant white suit with gold embroidery and a ton of jewelry. He wore more bling than a Hollywood pimp.

The last year had been a tough one for Terry, but four months since the completion of his cancer treatment, he looked to be on the mend.

Joe was also looking brighter, more like the boy she used to know. His face was fuller and his skin healthier. When she'd met him at Rockcliffe Manor last year, Max had recognized all the signs of an eating disorder. Somehow, he'd come out of that ordeal for the better. A survivor. Maybe not completely recovered, but he was over the worst of it. There was a vitality in his eyes, where there had been only hollowness before.

"So, are you boys each other's dates for the day?" she teased.

Terry rolled his eyes. "We're the fabulous singles, darling. We have to stick together, there are too many loved-up couples around, I'm afraid it could be catching. And I am too old for that malarkey."

"Anyone seen the happy couple yet?" Joe asked.

"I saw Daniel first thing this morning, but not since," Ben told him.

"They must be getting nervous about it now," Max said.

"No way," Ben said. "Not those two. After everything they've been through, getting married will be a breeze."

* * * *

Farther along the deck, out of sight of their guests, Daniel and Elijah stood side by side and gazed at the ocean, enjoying a moment of quiet before the ceremony kicked off. There were no nerves. No apprehension.

Their story had come full circle. It was only fitting that the next phase of their lives should begin here where it all began, onboard *The Atlantic Anthem*.

Despite almost drowning on that beach in Durham, Daniel had not lost his love for the ocean. When Elijah asked to marry him, there was only one place in the world Daniel wanted the service to take place. Here on this ship.

Breathing deep, he filled his lungs with the rich, salty air.

The two and a half years since they met had been a rollercoaster of huge peaks and incredible lows. Their lives had been at risk more than once, but they were still here. Survivors.

Although he had fully endorsed and cooperated with Keeley's book, Daniel had not read the finished product. He didn't need to. He had lived it. Muriel Durrell had spent her life consumed by hate and regret. He refused to do the same. The truth had been uncovered. That was enough.

Muriel had tried to kill him and she'd failed. When the news broke, Supporting Victims received more money in donations than they had in their entire history. Now Daniel was patron of the charity. He would continue to honor the victims of Oliver, Sonny and Muriel through his fundraising work.

Elijah took his hand, slipping his fingers between Daniel's, and brought it to his mouth. He kissed. "All right?"

"Perfect," Daniel answered.

They wore matching blue suits, with white silk shirts and red ties. Simple and classic. Elijah had never looked more handsome. Daniel had never felt happier. Fate had drawn them together and now they would be inseparable.

He would never know how Elijah summoned the strength to hold him afloat in the raging sea and pull him safely to the shore. The water could have claimed them both, but it hadn't.

They'd survived it together.

Daniel moved in for a real kiss. Deep and meaningful. He was the luckiest man in the world. And today, the world would know it.

The ship's wedding coordinator interrupted the kiss. "Are you guys ready?"

"Absolutely," they answered together.

Their family and friends were seated as they stepped out onto the terrace. Up front, Captain Roman Rassimov, resplendent and handsome in his naval uniform, waited to conduct the ceremony.

Hand in hand, Daniel Blake and Elijah Mann walked up the aisle. Heading into the future. Into a whole new life.

Daniel and Elijah — together they were unstoppable.

Want to see more from this author? Here's a taster for you to enjoy!

Silent Voices
Thom Collins

Excerpt

Josh Jackson didn't worry when his cousin failed to come home. It was Saturday night and Kevin was eighteen. Josh wasn't about to impose a curfew on the kid. Neither was he going to babysit. Kevin was old enough to take care of himself.

Josh checked Kevin's room when he came home from work at one o'clock. The spare bed hadn't been made since Kevin had gotten out of it that morning and yesterday's clothes were all over the floor — discarded jeans with his boxers still inside them, a scruffy T-shirt and a pair of dirty socks. The smell of the socks hit him from the doorway. Despite the reek of cheap deodorant and aftershave filling the room, the socks were pungent. *Teenagers*. Josh wasn't about to tidy up after him so he left things as they were, including the damp towel draped over the foot of the bed. The kid was only staying a few nights. If he wanted to live in a mess like that, so be it, so long as he left the place as he'd found it when he moved on.

Josh shut the door and went to bed. He wished his cousin luck. If the boy wanted to get laid, he'd rather he did it somewhere else. It was bad enough that Josh's lodger, Bobby, regarded the place as a Grindr pit stop, without his cousin treating it like a knocking shop, too.

Josh read for a while and half-listened for the sound of Kevin coming home, but eventually fell asleep.

He wasn't overly concerned in the morning to find Kevin's room just as he'd left it, though by now it smelled considerably worse. The fancy fragrances had worn off and all that remained was the fetid odor of teenage sweat and damp towel. *So, he stayed out all night. Good on him.* Josh had been a teenager once, a horny one at that, so he could totally relate. Kevin wouldn't get the chance to fuck around much when he was at home. His mother had very rigid views on that. It wouldn't have mattered whether Kevin had turned out straight or gay. His mother had raised a good boy and intended to keep him that way.

Kevin will be going back to her in a couple of days. He might as well have fun while the leash is off.

He was a good-looking lad. Josh knew he'd be popular in town. A little baby-faced for his age, but with the family features of blue eyes and blond hair, his fresh twinkie image would attract plenty of attention. He looked a lot like Josh had at that age. Josh had been a slim-looking twink until well into his twenties. It was only in the last few years he'd filled out with muscle and looked more like a man. The beard helped. How grateful he'd been when the ability to grow more than a few wisps of pale chin-fluff finally occurred. He kept it neat with a regular trim, but now that he had grown a beard, he couldn't ever see himself being without one.

Josh called Kevin's mobile while waiting for his morning coffee to brew. It rang a few times before going to voicemail. "Hi, it's me," he said. "Not checking up on you, I just want to know you're okay. Give me a ring back, or a text when you get this message. Just to say you're alive... Otherwise I'll have to call your mother," he added jokingly and hung up.

He had bigger concerns than a randy teenager. His restaurant, The Cellar Steps, was short on staff today and fully booked for both lunch and dinner. He'd asked all his remaining staff to come in early to help with the prep and service, which meant getting in even earlier himself. As the owner, it wasn't necessary, since he employed a manager for the day-to-day running, but Josh believed in setting an example from the top down. That meant rolling up his sleeves when things got tight. He thought about putting a little cash Kevin's way to help out, if he arrived home in decent time and wasn't too hung over.

He heard the heavy thud of the newspapers landing in the hall. *Perfect timing.* A little news and some freshly brewed coffee. A relaxing start to an otherwise hectic day.

Josh sat at the kitchen table with multiple Sunday supplements spread all around him when Bobby stumbled out of his bedroom in just his boxers and a T-shirt, yawning and scratching his belly and balls at the same time. His semi-hard dick waggled in the front of his shorts. Bobby lurched into the bathroom and returned a few minutes later, looking fractionally more awake, minus morning wood.

"Coffee?" Bobby asked. "Okay if I help myself?"

"You know where it is," Josh said, drawing back from the stench of alcohol that came off him in stale waves. "Jesus, your blood must be one hundred proof."

"I think I'm still drunk," Bobby observed. "The hangover hasn't kicked in yet."

"I don't envy you when it does."

"One cup of this and I'm crawling back beneath the duvet."

Josh looked at him uncertainly. An idea had just occurred to him. He hoped he was wrong. "I don't suppose my cousin is under that duvet with you?"

Bobby chuckled, his dark eyes crinkling. "Wouldn't that be something? He is kinda hot. But little blond cupcakes are not my thing. In Kevin's case, I could make an exception. Maybe."

"But did you?"

"Too close to home, bro. The kid's a cutie but he ain't worth the earache. I'd never hear the last of it."

It was some relief. Josh didn't have a problem with his young cousin fucking around — but with Bobby, no way. His lodger was a good friend but a total slut. Kevin would need a lot more experience under his belt before he was ready for that old hound. "I don't suppose you do know where he is? He hasn't been home."

"He's between somebody's sheets, all right. I walked into town with him last night, had a drink and showed him where to go."

"You left him on his own?"

"No, he left me. I guess I cramped his style. He headed off toward Gala Square with a group of studenty types. He didn't know how fast to ditch me once he got to talking to people his own age."

Josh loosened up again. He'd been right about Kevin. He knew what he was doing. A young man in a new city making friends fast. There was nothing to worry about.

* * * *

The lunch shift at The Cellar Steps was as frenzied as Josh had predicted. Sundays were always lively. He never had to worry about advertising the restaurant. It was the kind of place where, once people found it, they always came back. The main entrance was on Sadler Street in the center of Durham, close to the cathedral and castle entries. A low doorway on the ancient cobbled street led to a narrow stone staircase. First-time visitors were always excited by what they found below — a grand restaurant across two floors, built into the old cellars that dated back to the thirteenth century. The original stone arches and features survived, creating intimate dining alcoves. But it was the view that took people by surprise. From the upper floor, wide windows gave a magnificent view of the River Wear, which looped around the city.

Josh had fallen in love with the building the first time he had come here. It had taken three years of hard work to establish a reputation. The Cellar Steps was one of the few independent restaurants left in a city taken over by large chains. His chefs used the freshest local produce to create ever-changing, seasonal menus. The trick was to get people talking. Once word of mouth had spread, he had never looked back.

Sunday service was so busy that he didn't have a chance to worry about Kevin until things wound down around three-thirty. He helped his staff clear the tables, then left them to reset for the evening. Josh snagged his phone and climbed the steps to Sadler Street. Outside, he breathed in the fresh air. It was warm, but nothing compared to the heat of the packed restaurant. The glorious weather had drawn visitors to the city and the narrow street was thronged with people.

Josh studied his phone. Still no message from Kevin. Not even a text. *What is he playing at?* He dialed the boy's number. It went unanswered before again going to voicemail.

"C'mon, man, where are you? Drop me a line to say you're okay?"

Josh tugged at his bottom lip. He knew better than to worry. Kevin was an adult, and yet... Each year there were several untimely deaths in the river. Young kids, generally students, had too much to drink and sometimes tumbled into the unexpectedly fast-flowing currents. And it wasn't that long since a serial killer, The Durham Strangler, had preyed on young men in the area. Men like Kevin. No, he told himself, *you're fretting about nothing*. The Durham Strangler was dead and the river had been low all week. There had been no significant rain since June.

Still, once planted, the idea took root.

Josh called Bobby. "Has he come home yet?"

"Who?" Bobby grunted.

"Kevin. Who do you think?"

"No. Not heard him."

Josh sighed. "Check his room, will you?"

"I'm watching *Four in a Bed*," Bobby grumbled.

"Just do it," he snapped. He listened to the heavy-footed lumber as Bobby moved from the sofa to the spare bedroom.

"It's empty. Shit, man. Have you seen the state he's got this place in? He's only been here a few days and it looks like a crack house. It smells really rotten, too."

Something tightened in Josh's lower belly. "All right, now I'm worried. He's not answering his phone. Do you think I'm overreacting?"

"Dunno. I'd have thought he'd have the decency to stay in touch with the guy who's putting him up for free, but that's just me. He's a kid. Fuck knows what goes on in their heads."

"I was just thinking about, you know… The river. And the strangler from a few years back."

Bobby laughed. "Ooh, the drama!"

"I'm serious. What if something's happened to him and I've done nothing?"

"What's happened to him is that he's off his face on pills someplace. Or getting his brains fucked out. Or both."

"That doesn't make it better," Josh said.

"It's what kids do these days. Apparently."

"Damn. I need to find him." Josh paced the pavement. He'd never experienced this kind of responsibility, not for anyone. When Kevin had asked if he could stay a few days, he hadn't thought it would involve all this shit. Kevin had a place at Durham University, starting in September. He had said he wanted to check out the city and get a feel for it before his first term commenced. It had sounded like an innocuous request.

"When you called him, was his phone switched on or did it go straight to voicemail?" Bobby asked.

"No, it rang a few times first. Why?"

"GPS. If the phone is still on, you can track it."

"You're joking, right?"

"Nope."

"How?"

Fifteen minutes later, and with the help of Rachel, a nineteen-year-old kitchen assistant, Josh had downloaded an app to his smartphone and paid twenty pounds to register for an account with an online phone tracker.

"What? It's as easy as that? For twenty quid, I can find out where anyone is via their mobile phone? That's got to be a stalker's dream app." Josh stared at the screen. This couldn't be right. It was a huge breach of privacy. Maybe Kevin didn't want him to know where he was.

Then he should answer his bloody phone so I know he's alive.

Josh programmed Kevin's number into the app and hit Search.

The app tracked the handset to a position outside of the city. Josh began to doubt the accuracy of the system as he drove farther into the country. The landscape became more winding and rural with every mile. There had to be a mistake. Kevin wouldn't have come all this way for a one-night stand. Would he? As he navigated the route through a thickly wooded area, Josh pulled over to the side of the road and checked the phone number he had entered. Perhaps he'd miskeyed a single digit and was tracking somebody else's phone.

No. It was Kevin's number, all right. *Shit.* This made little sense. There was nothing to see on either side of the road, just dense forest. The trees overhung the road and formed a canopy that blocked out most of the afternoon sun. Josh's concern deepened. What if Kevin hadn't come here for a one-night stand? What if he had been forced against his will? What if he was already dead, lying in a ditch somewhere ahead?

No, Josh was being absurd. Bobby was right. He was a drama queen. Plenty of people from these rural areas came into Durham on the weekend. If Kevin had met someone he liked, there was every chance he would have gone home with them.

Josh checked the app again. It located the phone a little over a mile away. *What the hell?* He'd come this far. He drew the car back onto the road and followed the trace.

The tracker took him off the main road and down a track. The car jerked across the uneven trail, hardened after weeks of summer sun. He slowed to under fifteen miles an hour. He didn't want to fuck his suspension on top of everything else. Eventually the road widened again and he came upon a set of high, wrought-iron gates.

Josh got out of the car and approached the entrance. A red brick wall extended in both directions, tall and imposing. The message couldn't be clearer — keep out. There was a brass plaque mounted at the side of the gates. *Winterstone Grange.*

What the hell is Winterstone Grange? Josh had lived in Durham his whole life and hadn't heard of the place. It wasn't a hotel or spa. It had to be some kind of private estate. He pressed his face to the gates. A winding drive twisted through another area of woodland. Through a break in the trees, he made out a large manor house ahead. A long rectangular-shaped building with dozens of sash windows. There was an ornamental lake in front of the house.

What is Kevin doing in a place like this?

Uncertainly, he dialed Kevin's number again. It cut to voicemail after the customary few rings. He didn't bother with a message this time. The tracking app placed the phone within these walls. He wondered again how accurate the thing was. The website claimed it could trace a phone to within a hundred meters in urban areas, less so in rural spots. But he was hardly in the middle of nowhere. The city was less than ten miles away.

Kevin's phone was here.

Josh pressed the intercom on the wall. No answer. He jabbed the buzzer again, holding it longer. Still nothing.

What the hell?

Sign up for our newsletter and find out about all our
romance book releases, eBook sales and promotions,
sneak peeks and FREE romance eBooks!

https://totallyentwinedgroup.us7.list-
manage.com/subscribe/post

About the Author

Thom Collins is the author of Closer by Morning, with Pride Publishing. His love of page turning thrillers began at an early age when his mother caught him reading the latest Jackie Collins book and promptly confiscated it, sparking a life-long love of raunchy novels.

Thom has lived in the North East of England his whole life. He grew up in Northumberland and now lives in County Durham with his husband and two cats. He loves all kinds of genre fiction, especially bonkbusters, thrillers, romance and horror. He is also a cookery book addict with far too many titles cluttering his shelves. When not writing he can be found in the kitchen trying out new recipes. He's a keen traveler but with a fear of flying that gets worse with age, but since taking his first cruise in 2013 he realized that sailing is the way to go.

Thom loves to hear from readers. You can find his contact information, website details and author profile page at http://www.pride-publishing.com